GRIP

JIM IVY

GRIP
Copyright © 2019 by Jim Ivy.

All rights reserved. No part of this book may be reproduced in any form or by any electronic or mechanical means, including information storage and retrieval systems, without permission in writing from the publisher and author, except by reviewers, who may quote brief passages in a review.

This publication contains the opinions and ideas of its author. It is intended to provide helpful and informative material on the subjects addressed in the publication. The authors and publisher specifically disclaim all responsibility for any liability, loss, or risk, personal or otherwise, which is incurred as a consequence, directly or indirectly, of the use and application of any of the contents of this book.

ISBN: 978-1-951901-28-8 [Paperback Edition]
978-1-951901-29-5 [Hardback Edition]
978-1-951901-30-1 [eBook Edition]

I would like to give special thanks to friends and family who have helped and encouraged me with my first two books. Justin Hollie -Doris Wheelus-My wife Kimberly-My daughter Summer.

Thank you

CHAPTER 1

Arrived in a New City

Bryce helped his mother step out of his truck. The first thing he noticed was a smell of bagels and gasoline. The city walls were filled with graffiti. An old white sign with a painted arrow pointed the way to the Easy Sleep Motel. Earlier in the day a cab driver had recommended this motel to them. It was a dark alleyway. Even in the daytime, there was only one single light in the alleyway. It was lined with trash and smelled of urine. A homeless man was sleeping in a cardboard box. Bryce could only shake his head at his mother as they started down the alleyway. Suddenly, a tall man with braided hair and two gold teeth appeared. He had a slender frame, but his arms were tattooed and muscular. He stuck a gun into Bryce's face

Bryce's first response was to back off, but when they smacked his mother and told her to give them the damn money, Bryce snapped. He grabbed the hand with the gun in it and squeezed till the bones cracked into mush. The gunman screamed with pain. The other three thugs came at Bryce, screaming all the way, "We're going to beat you, man." The rage continued. Each thug's hand was turned into mush while they screamed with pain.

It wasn't over. Bryce had lost it. He started beating them with anything he could find. An old metal broom handle was lying in the alley. Bryce picked it up and started beating the men. There was such screaming that you could barely hear the sirens coming closer. One of the thugs got to his feet and ran out into the street, and Bryce followed him.

The police arrived. They came up from behind of Bryce. Bryce was beating the thug's broken body, pounding his head into a parked car. A police officer came from behind and yelled, "Freeze." Then the policeman made a mistake. He grabbed Bryce by accident. Bryce grabbed the policeman's hand and crushed it into Jell-O. He cried to his partner, "Help me!"

His partner, who was a veteran policewoman named Jaime, yelled, "Freeze!" She pulled her weapon.

Bryce turned for her. Their eyes locked as if they knew each other. A bittersweet memory from some twenty years ago. The rage was broken.

Bryce's mother yelled, "Don't shoot."

Bryce relaxed.

As other officers arrived, they placed him in handcuffs and put him in the squad car. The police were confused as to what was going on. They started talking to Bryce's mother even though she seemed dazed.

She told Jaime, "We are new in town looking for a cheap place to stay for six weeks while I have my treatment, but I guess we went on the wrong side of town because these four thugs attacked us, stole my purse, and hit me over the…" Then she paused and passed out.

The police started talking to witnesses while Jaime was trying to help Bryce's mother get to her feet. She collapsed in her arms. Hoping to find out more on the way to the hospital, Jaime chose to ride in the ambulance with Bryce's mother.

Bryce had been taken downtown. The police station was a madhouse. A drug ring had been busted, and every cell was full. Bryce was thrown in a cell to be dealt with later.

Police officer Jones was at the hospital getting his hand looked at. The doctor came back with the X-ray and told Jones, "It's not broken. You're lucky because the other three guys are all being put into casts, but you will have to wait a little while. One has a slight concussion and some cuts and scrapes, but you can take him."

*****

Meanwhile, Jaime was sitting at the bed of Bryce's mother waiting for her to wake up. She opened her eyes.

Jaime asked her, "Do you know where you are?"

"The hospital I think," Bryce's mother replied. "Where's Bryce? Where's my boy?"

"So that was your son?" Jaime said.

"Yes," she answered.

"They took him downtown," Jaime replied.

"For what, protecting me? What kind of town is this where they put innocent people in jail," replied Bryce's mother.

"He did assault a police officer," Jaime replied.

Bryce's mother said, "Those punks tried to rob me. When they hit me, that's when Bryce…"

"Calm down, ma'am. What's your name?" Jaime said.

"It's Amy Hix," she replied.

"And your son's name is Bryce Hix?" Jaime asked. "Bryce 'The Vice' Hix?"

"No one had called him that in almost twenty years," she replied.

The nurse came in to check her vital signs. Jaime stepped into the hallway and remembered back nineteen years ago.

*****

It was the Olympic trials, Jaime's brother, Randy, was in the finals against a sixteen-year-old phenom named Bryce Hix. Randy was a twenty-two-year-old senior in college, a heavy favorite to win. Randy had never lost a match in college. He was a three-time NCAA wrestling champion!

Jaime went to the restroom. There was a line out the door, but she really had to go bad, so she thought, *I'll go into the boy's because there's no line, and maybe no one's in there.*

JIM IVY

She went in, and four young men were standing there.

One started talking, "Well, look who's here. My dreams just came true."

Jaime tried to leave.

One of the young men stepped in front of the door and locked it.

Jaime said, "What are you doing? I'm getting out of here."

"No, you're not. You wanted to see the men's room, so we're going to show you what goes on in here," said one of the men.

Jaime started to scream.

One of the men grabbed her and shoved a tube sock in her mouth. As Jaime struggled, one of the bathroom stalls opened and a young man came out and said, "Let her go."

"Who's going to make me?" said one of the men.

"I am," said the young man.

"One against four, you've got to be kidding," said one of the men.

"I know you four pricks need a few more to make it even," the young man said.

The biggest punk stepped into the young man's face and said, "I know you. You're Bryce the Vice, the one everyone's talking about, but you don't look so tough to me."

Bryce said, "I can put you on your knees with just one hand, and if I do, you let her go and then apologize to her."

"Go for it," the man said.

In less than a split second Bryce grabbed him by the hand. The man started grimacing in pain and fell to his knees, frozen with pain.

Bryce said, "Let her go, apologize, and unlock the door."

The man followed Bryce's orders. While tears were running down the man's face, Bryce dragged him to the door. Then Bryce opened the door and said, "Get out of here, baby."

As Jaime went through the door, Bryce shut it behind her. Jaime heard some screaming and yelling, and then thirty seconds later Bryce appeared. He asked her if everything was all right.

She said, "Yes, thank you."

"Bullies. I hate them," Bryce said.

Then Bryce, while staring at his wrestling shoes and kicking the table, asked, "Will you watch me wrestle?"

She said, "Okay." She touched him on the hand and smiled.

He said, "It's on mat four in forty-five minutes, and after maybe we can get a burger. I've been starving myself for two weeks to keep my weight down."

*****

When the nurse came out of the room and said, "You can see her now," Jaime awoke from the trance she was in. Jaime went back into the room and asked Mrs. Hix, "Can you tell me what happened?"

"We were looking for a cheap place to stay for about six weeks because I have cancer and six weeks of treatment at the cancer clinic. A cab driver told us there were some cheap places," Mrs. Hix said.

"Yes, cheap and dangerous. There is a lot of crime and gangs down there. I can help you find a safer place to stay," Jaime said.

Jones walked in the room with a bandaged hand and said, "Jaime, are you done? We have to get back to the station because we've got a lot paperwork to do on those bozos and the asshole who damn near broke my hand!"

"That asshole is my son, and you're lucky he didn't break your hand," said Mrs. Hix.

"Calm down, Miss, I didn't mean anything by it," Jones replied.

"I'll come back by and see you before you check out. Here's my cell phone number, give me a call," Jaime said.

While driving back to the station, Officer Jones rambled on and on about what happened to him. Jaime just stared out the window remembering that day so long ago. Old feelings were coming back that she had suppressed. She wasn't even listening to Officer Jones.

*****

Meanwhile, Bryce was sitting in a holding cell with five other men. As he sat there, two other men were brought in. One of them was Jacko Colburt, leader of a local gang called Dogs. Each member was given names like Bulldog and Pit Bull. Jacko's name was Doberman. He had a bandage on his head, and his arm was in a sling. He walked up to a man sitting in a chair in the corner with his head bowed down and his hands folded across his head like he was asleep. Jacko kicked him in his work boots that he was wearing and said, "Get up, man, can't you see I need to sit down."

Bryce ignored him.

He kicked again. "Get up, man, before I throw you out."

A soft voice came from Bryce. "This isn't your day, is it?"

"What you say, little man?" Jacko said.

"I said, this isn't your day. You are about to get your ass kicked again by this little man," said Bryce.

As Bryce looked up, Jacko's eyes got as big as cue balls. He backed up as Bryce grabbed him by the good arm and squeezed. Jacko, screaming with pain, kicked and hit but couldn't shake free from his grip. The other men tried to break the grip as Jacko screamed in pain. Finally, the cell was opened. Three police officers raced in and sprayed Bryce with mace. Bryce broke loose. They took Jacko to another cell.

Jacko screamed at Bryce, "I'm going to get you, man. Your days are numbered. Nobody does that to me!"

Bryce went back into the corner, took his shirt, and wiped the mace out of his face.

*****

When Officer Jones and Jaime got back to the station, Bryce was already in the interrogation room. Two officers were talking to him.

"What's your name?" the officer asked.

"Bryce Hix," Bryce replied.

"What happened?" the officer asked.

Bryce took a deep breath, wiped his face with the towel that the officers provided for him, and sat back in his chair, looking all around, wishing he could start this day over again. In an instant his face turned to stone. He glared at the officers for a few seconds. The police officer for the first time felt fear as Bryce glared at him. One of them reached for his nightstick under the table.

Then Bryce said with a deep sigh, "My mother has cancer. We came here to get treatment for her. I asked the cab driver for directions for a cheap place to stay near the research cancer center. He suggested the Easy Sleep Motel. He gave me the address. I put it in my GPS and followed the directions. When we parked on the street. I felt uneasy, but my mother was always the optimist said, 'How bad could it be?' We followed the arrow that pointed the down the alleyway that was dark even in the daytime. Out of nowhere four men appeared, stuck a gun in my face, shoved my mother, and tried to take her purse. When they couldn't get it loose from her grip, one of them punched her in the face. Pretty much everything after that is a blur."

"Do you know that one of the men you assaulted was a police officer?" the officer asked.

"No, I didn't. He grabbed me, and he paid the price! I was in a rage, and I thought it was one of them," Bryce replied. "Where's my mother? Is she all right?"

"We'll talk about your mommy later." One of the officers smirked.

Bryce had a steel coffee mug in his hand. He glared at the officer and said, "When you speak of my mother, you speak of her with respect." Bryce set the cup down. It was squished like play dough.

"Take it easy. You've got some grip there," said the officer.

"So they tell me," Bryce replied.

Jaime and Officer Jones were watching through the glass. The officers continued their investigation.

"So, Mr. Hix, why are you here?" said the officers.

"My mother has cancer, and she is here for treatment. It's supposed to last six to eight weeks. A cabbie told us there were cheap rooms down there, but I guess that's not a good neighborhood," replied Bryce. "If I have to keep repeating myself over and over again, I'm never going to get out of here."

The officer asked, "What do you do for a living?"

"I'm a brick mason," said Bryce.

"So is that why you have such a strong grip?" the officer asked.

Bryce replied, "No, let's just say I was born that way."

"What do you mean by that?" asked the officer.

"I really don't think that's any of your business. What's that got to do with my mother being hit and robbed?" Bryce replied.

"Look, we're just trying to get the mental picture here, and we don't need any smartass remarks," the officer said.

Bryce replied, "Okay. I have two tendons in my right hand and three in my left. You only have one. My grip is God's gift and God's curse. When I'm angry or keyed up, I have a hard time controlling it. That's why all those punks are hurting now!"

The officer said, "What about Officer Jones?"

Bryce said, "Well, let's just say he was an innocent victim, much like my mother. I am sorry he got hurt."

The officer asked, "What about the female police officer?"

Bryce said, "For one thing, she is a woman and something seemed familiar about her eyes."

The officer replied, "We are still going to have to hold you till we get this figured out. It is really up to Officer Jones if he wants to press charges or not. We'll put you in a better cell and isolate you from other prisoners."

Bryce stood up from table. He said to the officer, "I'm a little confused. I've been sitting here for an hour talking about me. What about those bastards that mugged us and hit my mother? You haven't asked me about filing charges on them. So what's going on with them?"

The other officer paused and looked at the other before saying, "A mistake was made. We had to let them go."

Bryce shouted, "What mistake?"

The officer threw up his hands and said, "In all the confusion over what had happened, an officer forgot to give them their Miranda rights and they have a lawyer on retainer so we had to let him go."

Bryce shouted again, "You got to be kidding. How stupid is the police in this town? That's the first thing they did to me when they put me in the police car."

The police officer shouted back, "Look, they all thought you were the criminal and they were the victims because you had injured a police officer and was out of control!"

Jaime turned to Officer Jones and said, "You can't charge him. It was an accident. You heard him."

"Bullshit, look at my hand. It's mush. Somebody's going to pay, and it's going to be him. Whose side are you on? This man hurt me, and you're taking his side. I'm your partner and your superior officer. I'm beginning to worry where your loyalties lie," Officer Jones replied. He glared at her for a few seconds, then threw up his hands and stormed out of the room.

Jaime looked on with disgust with her partner, and she decided to go see her brother.

Jaime's brother's name is Randy Bell, Olympic wrestling champion. He won two gold medals and never lost a match. He had his own wrestling school where he trained Olympic hopefuls. Convincing Randy wouldn't be easy, but he is still well respected in the city. He even has his name on the water tower. It says, "The home of the two-time Olympic gold medalist Randy Bell."

CHAPTER 2

Trying to Help

Jaime walked into the gym.

Randy shouted across the room, "It's a raid. The cops are here!"

Jaime replied, "Yeah, I'm here to arrest you." As she hugged him, she said, "Hi, brother, guess who we arrested today?"

"Dad," Randy replied as he chuckled.

"No." Jamie paused before saying Bryce's name. Looking deep into the eyes of her brother, she said in a soft voice, "Bryce Hix."

He stepped back, shook his head, and said, "I'm not surprised. He was a punk."

Jamie answered with her voice cracking, "He was the only guy who ever beat you."

"Yeah, he cheated. He was drugged up and disqualified. Look, I know you had some kind of crush on him, but that was nineteen years ago. Can't you see him for what he is, a cheater and a liar."

"He claimed somebody tampered with his drug test because he never used drugs."

"That's my sister. She believes everyone," Randy said. "Can we put this to rest? He was arrested today. He's a punk, and he'll always be a punk. Even Dad said he saw him putting something in his water bottle during the match."

Jamie replied, "Dad, he was so pissed off because you lost. He would have said anything to get him disqualified. He dang near punched the referee, and you're dream of going to the Olympics was over. If he doesn't get disqualified."

Randy replied, "You're kidding me, right?" He shook his head. He can't believe he was having this conversation with his sister.

Jamie's voice cracked even more when she said, "But he needs help."

"You're not suggesting I bail him out."

"Yes," Jaime replied.

"You're nuts. I would do anything for you, but you're crazy. I'm not spending a dime on him."

Jamie and Randy's father walked up. His name was Rock Bell. He chimed in, "What's going on?"

"Father, your daughter is nuts. She wants me to bail out Bryce Hix. What do you think about that?"

Rock said, "Are you kidding? What's he doing here?"

Jamie said, "He was arrested for defending his mother in a robbery attempt."

Rock said. "Then why was he arrested?"

"He hurt my partner by mistake," Jamie said.

"He hurt Jonesy, and you want me to bail him out. You've lost your mind."

Jamie responded, "His mother has cancer. The thug punched her, putting her in the hospital, and now nobody can get him out." As she stormed out of the gym, she screamed, "You've got the money. Help them out."

Randy looked at Rock and said, "PMS?"

"I guess," Rock replied. "I never saw her act like this before. She has always been in such control. Now she looks out of control."

Randy shook his head and told Rock he would be back later. After all, Randy loved his sister. Something was going on, so he had to see for himself.

*****

Meanwhile, back at the precinct, about two hours later, an officer came to the cell Bryce was in.

"You've got a visitor. Come with me."

He took him to the visitation room. He sat down and handcuffed him. Bryce stared at the glass, and in walked Randy Bell.

Bryce said, "Shit, what the hell do you want?"

Randy answered, "I had to see you. Somebody wants me to bail you out, and I want you to tell me why I should."

Bryce glared at Randy for a second or two, then said, "I don't want jack shit from you."

As Randy stood up to walk out, he looked back at Bryce and said, "You could've been great. Why did you cheat?"

Bryce yelled back at him, "Ask your father. He knows the truth, and if you don't, you better ask him why he ruined my life so his son could be an Olympic champion. And I can't get out of here to see how my mother is. What's fair about that? What's fair about that?"

Randy slammed the door behind him. Randy left the precinct and went back to the gym to find his father. When Randy arrived at the gym, he walked in to his office. His father was sitting at his desk. Rock looked up and said, "Where have you been?"

Randy answered, "I went to the police station. I was going to bail Bryce out."

Rock shouted, "Bryce! You mean Bryce Hix. Now who is nuts?"

Randy said, "I didn't know what I was doing there. I just hoped I would maybe see what Jamie sees, but all I saw was a bitter man blaming everyone else for his problems."

*****

Meanwhile back at the hospital, Jaime walked in to Mrs. Hix's room.

"How are you feeling, ma'am?"

"I feel a little better. Do you know where my son is? I'm worried about him."

Jamie answered, "He is still in a holding cell. Don't worry about him, he will be safe. He did assault a police officer. They set his bail at $5,000."

"Five thousand dollars!" she yelled. "How can I pay that? It will wipe us out. The money we have is supposed to last us for my eight weeks of treatment."

Jamie leaned over and took her hand and said, "I have already talked to the research hospital. They said they are going to admit you, and you can start your treatment. I know a place where your son can stay for a while till this charge is dropped."

"Why are you doing this, dear?" she said.

"Let's just say he helped me out once, and I'm returning the favor," Jamie said.

Mrs. Hix answered, "Bryce will never do it. He's too proud of a person."

"But maybe if you talk to him, he will do it," Jamie said. "I don't know if he finds out who I am, he will probably never speak to me again."

Mrs. Hix looked puzzled and asked, "What do you mean, who are you?"

"My brother is Randy Bell, and my father is Rock Bell. I know this is very awkward, but I had nothing to do with the wrestling thing. And I really don't understand the hatred that are between them!"

Mrs. Hix answered, "Bryce never cheated or used drugs a day in his life. Someone spiked his water bottle. That's why he tested positive for drugs. He beat your brother fair and square."

Jamie answered back, "I was there. I was filming the match for my dad. I was pulling for Bryce to win because I had a little crush on him. My brother and father never knew that I had met Bryce earlier."

Mrs. Hix said, "How did Bryce help you out how?"

"I have never spoke of this before today. I was almost raped in the boy's bathroom. Bryce broke it up and got me out of there without being harmed. He asked me to watch him wrestle. I never knew he was wrestling my brother till it started. He smiled and winked at me before the match started, and after he had won, though I was happy for him, I couldn't see him after the match because my father and brother were so upset after Bryce beat my brother. My father was so angry and started saying things that he had cheated, even got into a shouting match with his coach. They were nose to nose, yelling at each other. How could I now congratulate Bryce. I was fifteen years old. I didn't know what to do. I left the camera there and hid in the background."

"I could see Bryce looking through the crowd. Maybe he was looking for you, but at the time I felt he was looking for me," Mrs. Hix said. "So you're her? The girl he wouldn't leave till he had seen you again. He stayed till all the matches were over hoping to see you again."

Jamie answered, "I'm so sorry I wanted to see him. I just couldn't."

Mrs. Hix smiled, squeezing Jamie's hand. "I think I understand. Maybe you should talk to him, and it wouldn't hurt if you shed a few tears. He melts when that happens."

Jamie smiled and said, "You're so bad!"

She answered, "I just know my boy."

*****

Jamie then hurried back downtown to the courthouse where Bryce was being formally charged before the judge. Jamie walked into the courtroom. Bryce was sitting down. He was handcuffed. The judge was looking over the notes in the case.

Suddenly, Bryce saw Jamie, and his heart was in his throat. He said to himself, "It's her. What's she doing here?"

The judge was a real hardliner. No messing around. When he banged his gavel, he did it with authority. He then cleared his throat and said, "Bryce Hix, please stand. You are being charged with assaulting a police officer. What do you have to say for yourself?"

Bryce said, "Your Honor, my mother and I was being assaulted by five punks. It was an accident how the police officer was injured."

The judge butted in, "An accident? You almost broke his hand, then nearly choked him. It seems to me you were out of control. I am not happy with this. Your bail is set at $5,000. Do you have it?"

Bryce said, "Yes."

"Then pay the court clerk. Your hearing will be set in two weeks from today. My suggestion is for you, young man, get an attorney."

The bailiff took the handcuffs off Bryce, then led him to the clerk's office to pay the bail. Jamie followed behind them. Bryce kept looking back behind him. As Bryce paid the bail, Jamie came up to him and said, "We need to talk. Let's go sit in my car."

Bryce said, "I'd really like to talk to you, but I need to find out how my mother is and or where she is."

Jamie said, "Your mother is fine. They're moving her to the cancer research center. They are going to let her stay at the center."

Bryce looked puzzled and said, "How did that happen?"

She said, "I pulled a few strings. I know the CEO of the research center."

As Bryce listened, all he could do was look at Jamie up and down. How beautiful she was. She really hadn't changed at all in his eyes. He finally said, "Thank you. Can you take me there?"

She nodded and said, "Yes."

But Bryce said, "I feel I have a few things to say to you. It's been almost twenty years since I've seen you, but I waited for you after the match. I just figured you had to leave with your parents. I didn't even know your last name or how to get in touch with you." Bryce started stuttering a little, searching for the right words to say.

Finally, Jamie blurted out, "My brother is Randy Bell. My father is Rock Bell."

The smile was erased from Bryce's face.

Jamie kept going, her voice racing. "I was so glad when you won," she said as she searched for the right words.

"I understand. You felt pity on me and that's why you helped me and my mother," Bryce said smugly.

"No, no!" she said.

His anger was growing inside. All the old wounds were opening up—the pain, the disgrace of being accused of using drugs to enhance his performance.

Jamie then grabbed him by the arm and looked deep into his eyes. She said, "Look at me, and you'll know the truth. Look into my eyes, feel my heart beating. You're the only man I ever felt like this before." Her voice was cracking, and she tried not to cry, but the emotion of the moment got the best of her. She just hugged him and held him with all of her being.

He could feel the warmth of her body pressed against him. At first he was not trying to pull away. Bryce let his guard down just for a brief moment and hugged her back. She felt this as a single tear trickled down his face. They held each other, not saying a word for nearly thirty seconds. They then let each other go, neither wanting to look into each other's eyes.

Jamie said, "Where are you going to stay?" She wiped the tears out of her eyes, her voice still cracking with emotion.

He said, "I don't know, I've spent all our money to get out of jail."

Jamie looked into his eyes and said, "I have a very comfortable couch. You can stay with me until—"

Bryce interrupted, "Wait, wait, wait, you want me to stay with you?"

"Yes," she said.

"Your old man and brother would shit a brick if I stayed with you," he said.

"Let me worry about that!" she said.

He answered, "Well, maybe I can get a job or pay your rent till I get a few paychecks."

Jamie just nodded.

As they got into her car and drove to see his mother, he asked her if she thought his truck was still where he parked it.

She said, "No, I had it towed to the police station. It would be safer there."

"Boy! You really taken care of everything, haven't you?"

"By the way, what do you do for a living?" she said.

He said, "I'm a brick mason."

"Hey! I know a guy!"

He just shook his head and smiled as they left, driving to the cancer center where his mother was.

*****

Meanwhile, back at the police station, Officer Jones was typing out his police report one handed.

Another officer came behind him and said, "I checked out Brice Hix like you told me to. He does have a couple of prior arrests. One was he broke a guy's hand trying to steal some tools of his. He was not convicted of that. The other one was eighteen years ago. He assaulted a woman. The father of the girl pressed charges. He spent six months in county. He admitted it. And here are some pictures of the girl."

Jones said, "Look at all those bruises on that poor girl. He really messed her up, and that does it for me. I'm pressing full charges. I don't care what Jamie says."

Jones got in his car and went to the gym where Randy and his father were.

Randy yelled out, "Hey, Jones, you all right?"

"Yes," he replied.

Randy said, "That guy has some grip, huh?"

"Oh yeah, it hurt like hell. I thought my hand was in a vice, and I just stood there paralyzed. Where's Jamie?" he said.

"I don't know, I thought she was with you at the station."

"She had the nerve to ask me to help that guy."

Randy said, "I know, she has sympathy for this guy."

"I don't get it. Looked at this." Jones handed Randy the file on the Bryce.

Randy looked on in horror as he read the file. He kept shaking his head and talking to himself, "This guy is bad news. I need to get her away from this nut."

"Maybe if you, me, and Rock talk to her, she will listen," Jones said.

Randy folded his arms and nodded his head up and down. "Maybe," he replied. "Maybe. She's pretty stubborn like Dad."

"You mean, exactly like Rock. They are both always right, even if you prove them wrong," Jones said. "I have called her three times on her cell phone, and she won't answer, and another thing, the guy he worked over is the kind you don't mess with. He will wind up floating face down in the river. We need to keep her away from him for her own protection."

Rock walked up to where Jones and Randy were talking.

"What's up?" he said.

"We are just talking about Jamie, and maybe if we all talked to her she will just leave him alone and get on with her life. It's like he has some hold over her."

Rock interrupted, "Wait a minute, is she with him?"

"I don't knowI can't find her," Jones said.

"Why don't we just leave this guy alone? He has obviously had a tough time in his life. I think we all need to stay away from him, and maybe if we help him out, the quicker he will get out of town."

"Pop!" Randy yelled out. "You're kidding, right? This guy is a bitter man whose life didn't turn out the way he wanted it to. He blames everyone else but himself. He then laid some blame on you." Randy pointed at Rock.

Rocks eyes went big, then his voice trembled, "What did he say?"

"He said you knew something about his drug test or something like that. I just shrugged it off."

Rock said, "You did the right thing. Where do you think Jamie is? Do you think she is with him?"

"I'm going to find her and talk to her. Maybe we should all go," Jones said.

"No," said Rock. "Let me talk to her first."

Rock walked away with his car keys in hand. He was going to the cancer treatment center to see if Jamie was there.

Randy tugged Jones on the shirtsleeve. "Let's go to her place and wait for her there. I have a key to get in, and we will wait for her and show her the file, and maybe she'll listen if Dad doesn't get through to her."

They went out the back to Randy's car, driving away. Officer Jones went on and on how bad Bryce was when Randy shouted at him, "Just drop it, dude. The girl doesn't want to date you anymore. Get that through your dumb cop head. You're not gonna like any, dude, she does. And this one I happen to agree with you, so quit trying to sell me. I'm on your side, and if we get her away from him, that doesn't mean she's going back to you. She doesn't love you, man!"

They sat in silence the remainder of the drive to Jamie's place.

*****

Rock pulled up to the cancer center and walked to the front desk to inquire about what room Bryce's mother was in. After sweet talking the lady at the information desk, Rock got the room number and headed for the elevator. He then arrived at the floor. The elevator door opened, and he walked down the hall, looking for the right room number. Then there it was. The door was cracked open. He peeked through the crack to see if anyone was there.

A woman was lying, quietly watching TV. She suddenly turned to the door and said, "Are you coming in, or are you just going to stare at me?"

Rock kinda laughed and walked into the room.

Mrs. Hix said, "Do I know you?" as she squinted at him to get a better look at him.

He answered, "I don't think so. I'm looking for the lady police officer named Jamie."

She answered, "She went with my son to get me some ice cream. She's a lovely caring person. They seem to go together, don't you think?"

The thought of Jamie and Bryce being together turned his stomach, but he did not want her to know this.

He then asked, "What are you in for? If you don't mind me asking."

She said, "Well, I have cancer, and I'm here for treatment. Hopefully, it works and I will have more time."

He said, "You seem so cheerful for someone under…" He then lost his train of thought and continued, "I lost my wife to cancer twenty-five years ago." His lips quivered.

She replied, "I'm sorry, dear, for your loss of your wife. But I'm not going to give up or shut down. I'm going to live and fight. I've done it my whole life, and I am not going to stop now. This is just a small detour, a bump in the road."

Rock smiled and said, "You're a tough old broad. What about your husband?"

She sighed and said, "He died over thirty years ago. He was a rat and abusive man. The world is a better place without him."

Rock stepped back, trying to take in what she just said. Mrs. Hix was so confident and truthful. He could tell she truly believed what she said. She reminded him of his wife. Tough and truthful. He then apologized and said he had to leave. He asked Mrs. Hix to tell Officer Bell to call him. He hesitated, then he stepped out of the room. A small tear trickled down his face. He couldn't help but like her. She was so much like his wife, it was scary, he thought. He walked to the elevator and went back to the gym. He needed time to figure out what he was going to say to Jamie the next time he saw her.

*****

A few minutes passed, and Jamie and Bryce arrived in Mrs. Hix's room with the ice cream. It was fudge ripple, her favorite.

"Here you go, Mother," he said.

"Jamie," she said, "a man was here looking for you. He didn't leave his name, but we had a nice conversation and then he left. He also said how he lost his wife twenty-five years ago."

Jamie nodded her head while biting her lip, knowing it was her father. She thought, *Should I say who it was, or should I just wait? I really don't know how both of them will react.* She then stood up nervously. "I have to go. I have to meet this guy. I forgot all about it."

She handed Bryce her key and the directions to her house. Backing out the room, she said, "Just make yourself at home. I got to run." She waved at both of them and hurried out of the room down the hall to the elevator.

Bryce sat down next to his mother. She had a big smile on her face.

"Her place?" she said.

"Well, she's letting me stay there since I had to spend our money on bail, and she got me some work with some homebuilder she knows. It's two weeks' work, but at the least I will make a little money."

His mother then asked, "You're not going to be here with me."

"Mom, I had to make some money to pay my debts. I'm sorry I can't be here 24/7. I didn't plan on being mugged!"

"Okay," she said. "Calm down." She then ran her hand over his head back and forth, rubbing gently. She then said, "So you're staying with her?" Her eyes were wide open and smiling.

"In separate rooms," he replied, shaking his head back and forth with his mouth wide open.

She winked at him and said, "Right, right!" while smiling.

"Mom, you have such a dirty mind." He smiled back at her.

"No, I see the way she looks at you, and I know what it means."

"Well, I wish someone would tell me what she's thinking and what she wants because I don't know," he replied, rolling his eyes.

"Isn't it obvious, son? She wants you!"

*****

Jamie arrived at the gym looking for her father. When he wasn't there and she couldn't find Randy, she thought, *Crap, they're at my place. Hopefully, Bryce won't be there.* She hurried back to her car.

Ten minutes later she arrived at her place and opened the door. Officer Jones and Randy were sitting at the kitchen table.

"Hi, sis."

"Hi, partner."

They spoke in unison.

"What are you doing here?" she asked.

"We came over to talk to you about Hix."

Jamie's eyes rolled. She took a deep breath and said, "Hand over my key. I don't want you popping in any time you damn well feel like. Hand it over. Hand it over now!"

"Oh, sis, just chill out and listen. Bryce has a record. I think you should look at before you make any judgment on him."

"Out," she said, pointing toward the door.

Jones stood up and shouted, "You're going to I'll listen and see this file if I have to cuff you to the bedpost."

Jamie was pissed standing there, biting her lip, shaking her head back and forth. She said, "Okay, I will look at it." She grabbed it out of Jones's hand, laid the file down on her kitchen table, opened it, and started reading.

Jones blurted out, "He sexually abused a young girl, spent six months in jail, and admitted to it without a denial!"

She answered, "I thought you wanted me to read this, so why don't you guys leave. I'll read this and make up my own mind, okay? Just go!"

"But, sis!" Randy said.

"Out!" she said as she pointed to the door.

As they both were leaving, Jones said, while walking out the door, "I'm still going to charge his ass. I don't care what you say!"

Jamie then angrily slammed the door behind them, walking back over to her kitchen table. She sat down she opened up the file again and read it page by page, then she came to the pictures of the young girl. The bruises were deep purple on the young girl. She could not help but tear up a little for the young girl. She thought, *How could this man do this?* She slammed the file on the table. Jamie then started pounding her head on the kitchen table. Then her doorbell rang. Jamie looked at her front door and could see it was her father.

Jamie yelled at the door, "Go away, Dad. I want to be alone."

Her father started pounding on the door.

Jamie came to the door and opened it, standing in the doorway with her arms crossed. She said, "You're not going to jump on me too, are you?"

He said, "No, I'm not. I just wanted to know what you're thinking about him."

Jamie responded sarcastically, saying that his name was Bryce. She just sighed and said, "I don't know. I just don't know what I'm feeling, but something is there. I feel it in my heart."

As her father listened to her, he could see it in her eyes that she was feeling something. He asked, "What is it about him that you like? How do you even know him?"

She said, "I never told you this before, what happened about an hour before Randy and Bryce wrestled that day. I went to the bathroom."

He said, "I remember that you came back all flustered and upset. You said it was a madhouse at the bathroom."

"Well, Father, this is what really happened…" She told him the story how she ended up in the boy's bathroom and was held against her will by four young men that were threatening her of rape, and out of the blue a young man saved her, and it was Bryce. "He saved me—and possibly being raped by three or four young men. It was Bryce Hix. He took charge, got me out of there without being hurt. That's why, Dad. Do you understand now why he has a special place in my heart?" she said with quivering lips and tears in her eyes.

Her father looked at her in disbelief and then hugged his daughter.

The doorbell rang again.

Jamie pulled away from her father and said under her breath, "This better not be Jones or Randy."

It was Bryce this time. He stood outside the door, nervously spinning the key around his finger, wondering if he should go on in.

Jamie walked over to the door and looked out the peephole. She could see it was Bryce. She turned to her father and said, "What do I do?"

Her father started stuttering, "Let him in. It will be okay."

She whispered, "I don't know how he will react seeing you here."

He said, "Just get it over with. Let him in. I will keep my cool, I'll be friendly."

She opened the door. Bryce was standing there with a small suitcase and a smile.

"Sorry," he said, "I came a little early. I really need to take a shower. I smell something awful." He came in the door. He spotted her father. "Oh, I'm sorry, I must've come at a bad time."

Rock said, "That's okay. I was just leaving." He kissed Jamie and started for the door but then stopped and extended his hand toward Bryce.

Bryce paused. He stuck his hand out but then pulled back.

Rock just nodded and walked out the door, shutting it behind him.

Jamie glared at Bryce and said, "How could you do that?"

Bryce said, "Wait a minute, you don't understand! I can't just forgive everything."

Jamie snapped back, "My father extends his hand, and you don't shake it! I know you blame him for your loss. Maybe my brother is right about you. He showed me your file and how you sexually abused a woman and went to jail for six months. The pictures tell the whole story. How can you explain this to me? I want to believe you."

His face turned red with anger. His voice had a very bitter tone. "What do you want to hear, Jamie? You want to know the truth! I'll tell you the truth! Just shut up and listen. Give me two minutes, and I will be out of here. You don't know me. You don't know what it's like to be me. I have never intentionally hurt anyone, including Mary, the girl you're talking about. She was my first real girlfriend. We were making out in my car. She started touching me, so I started touching her. As we went at it, she was moaning with pleasure, or so I thought. I didn't know I was hurting her. She never said it hurt. I couldn't tell when I get worked up, I can't feel how much pressure I was putting on her breasts and other parts of her body. You don't know what it's like to not know if you're hurting someone, not to ever be able to touch a woman's body because you're afraid you will hurt them or shake someone's hand. I can't control this grip of mine. That's why I have no wife, no girlfriend, no life. I thought you were different. That maybe you were seeing the real me. That young man you met twenty years ago, that's me. I'm not the monster Mary's father made me out to be. Do you think I'm not afraid it would kill me if I hurt you? I won't let that happen. Maybe I should just go. Who are we kidding anyway? We can't go back." He started for the door. He went out the door and pulled it behind him.

Jamie had so many feelings and doubts, she didn't know what to do. She looked at her door knob. It was crushed. "Wow," she said to herself.

*****

Bryce went back to the hospital and slept in the parking lot in his truck. He looked in his wallet. All he had was $153. He knew he would have to find work somewhere. He didn't know if the brick job Jamie had gotten him would still be there now.

The next morning Bryce was sitting up in his truck. He woke up early, and when the sun came up, he opened the door and stretched his arms and legs. He had a hard time getting the stiffness out from sleeping in his truck. He then walked into the cancer treatment center to see his mother. When he arrived at his mother's room, he pushed open the door very quietly. His mother was still sleeping. He then slipped into her bathroom. He locked the door behind him. He took his clothes off and turned the shower on. It would feel good to try scrub the jail scent off his body. When finished, he turned the shower off, grabbed a towel, and started drying off. He heard the door open to his mother's room. He quietly put fresh clothes on, trying to listen for who it was. As he turned the water off, he heard the door open to his mother for us to try to be quiet not knowing who it was.

It was Jamie. She came into the room and gently tried to wake Bryce's mother. She finally woke up, and Jamie said, "Have you seen Bryce?

She answered, "No, I haven't seen him. I thought he was with you?"

A worried look came over Jamie. "I just thought he would be here," Jamie said. "Bryce needs to call me as soon as he can. This morning, if at all possible."

As Jamie started to leave, Mrs. Hix asked, "What happened?"

Jamie turned and sat back down beside her bed. She was upset, but she started talking anyway.

"Bryce came over to my place. It wasn't good. I said some things, some hurtful things about his past. He then opened up to me, told me what happened, and I let him go without saying a word. I think I hurt him. Can you help me? Tell me what happened with the girl he sexually assaulted."

She said, "Did he tell you what happened?"

"Yes," Jamie replied.

"Then that's what happened. Bryce doesn't lie. It was an accident. Mary's father pushed for the assault charge. Bryce was so ashamed, he didn't even put up a fight. He had hurt someone he cared about. It devastated him. He pleaded guilty and did his six months. He was sorry. He paid his debt, and he has never dated or loved anyone since. He can't control his hands, with the pressure of his grip, when he gets excited or mad. The older he got, the worse it got. It finally got a job as a brick mason's helper, and a year or two later, he went out on his own. He was really fast and in demand back home. He could break the bricks with his hands."

At that moment Jamie's cell phone rang. She handed Mrs. Hix a business card with her cell phone number on it. She pointed to the back of the card. The number of the homebuilder was on it. "Have him call me, please." She then stepped outside in the hall to answer her phone. It was Jones, her partner.

He sarcastically said, "Nice to know you're still alive!"

"I've been a little busy," she answered.

He said, "Are you with him?"

She said, "No."

"We need to find him. One of our informers let us know the word is out that the dogs are coming for your friend. The guys he roughed up were let out about thirty minutes ago."

"You're kidding!" she yelled.

Jones then told her, "They made bail, and the word on the street is that they are coming for him to settle the score. He needs to be warned, and you need to stay away from him, so you don't get popped too. He's dead and don't even know it yet!"

Jamie said, "We have to protect him. I'll go to the captain!"

He said, "We don't have the manpower to protect a damn tourist. Besides, he'll be in jail anyway in a couple weeks, if he lives that long."

"Screw you, Jones." She hung up the phone. Jamie then decided to go see the captain. She had to do something. Jamie drove quickly to the station. She stormed into her captain's office. He was sitting at his desk looking over some police reports, never looking up at her.

He said, "I didn't hear you knock, Officer Bell." He continued writing.

Jamie blurted out, "Captain, we have to protect Bryce Hicks. The dogs have put out a hit on him."

The captain still never looked up and said, "Bryce Hicks. Isn't he the guy who injured your partner, Officer Jones. Sounds like a criminal to me, and I don't protect criminals. I protect our citizens. End of story. Get out my office."

Jamie pulled out her badge and tossed it on the desk and said, "I quit." She started out of her captain's office.

He raised his head up, took his glasses off, and shouted, "Stop. Turn around."

Jamie did, glaring at her captain.

He sat back in his chair and said, "What would you like me to do? Jamie, your partner has already filed charges on him. He told me you had some kind of emotional attachment to this guy when you were a kid, but I'm not going to lose one of my best officers over this crap."

Jamie just stared at him and didn't say a word.

Finally, the captain said, "Give his address to the duty sergeant, and we will send a patrol car wherever he is, at least once every couple of hours. That's the best I can do."

Jamie nodded her head and started out the door.

The captain shouted at her, "You forgot this." He tossed her badge back to her.

Jamie caught it as she left the captain's office. She said sarcastically, "Thanks, Captain."

******

Back in the hospital room, Bryce opened the door. His mother was surprised to see him.

She said, "How long you been in there?"

He replied, "About twenty minutes. I took a shower."

Mrs. Hix crossed her arms and gave Bryce a sympathetic look. "So did you hear everything?" she asked.

He said, "Pretty much.

"Then why did you let her go?" she asked.

"Mom, it's just better this way. It's just too complicated. So gave me the card with the number I need to work."

She then said, clutching his hand, "Son, you just can't work when things get tough. It's time you made a life for yourself. I won't be around forever. I would like to see you happy before I die, not just working all the time to fill the void in your life, and maybe have a grandchild."

Bryce said, "Mom, stop saying you're going to die. You're going to live, and I'm going to work so we can live here just long enough to get you well. Then we will go home." He bent down and gave his mother a kiss on the cheek and was out the door.

When Bryce got to his truck he called the number Jamie had left for him. The man who answered was Earl Nixon, a homebuilder. They talk for a few moments, and he told Bryce, "You're getting this job or the recommendation of police officer Jamie Bell. I trust her. If she says you're trustworthy, then that's good enough for me." He gave Bryce the address and directions how to get to the job site. "My foreman will meet you there and get you started. I pay once a week on Friday."

Bryce then hurried to the job site. He pulled in and asked for the foreman. He introduced himself. They walked over to the house, and he said, "Look, our other brick mason is on vacation. He'll be back in two weeks. I only have one helper for you. His name is José. He speaks some English. With one helper, this will probably take you two weeks. I have two other houses, but he should be back when you get done."

Bryce asked, "If I get this one done, can I have the other two houses?"

The foreman and looked puzzled said, "Sure."

Bryce said, "I'll hold you to that if José can keep up."

CHAPTER 3

Dogs' Planned Revenge

At a secret location called the Dog Pen, the members of the gang called the Dogs were all in attendance. When Jacko Colbert, or his dog name Doberman, calls for meeting, everyone is there. The dog pen is a large basement in an old vacant warehouse. It has several secret entrances and is powered by generators. They have an illegal gas line running from a nearby factory that ran the generators. It also has underground parking. The dogs promised the factory owner protection from theft. Also, that he keeps quiet to the police. If he ever told the police, he knew his life and his family would be in danger. The dogs always had a patrol on lookout on the factory.

It was a dark cool night. Jacko Colbert, whose dog name was Doberman, stood in the middle of the room with a broken hand, his arm in a sling, and his eye swollen shut. There was anger in his voice as he spoke.

"Look at me. No one does this to us. One thing the dogs has is respect from the police, from rival gangs, and the people of this city. They fear us. They don't mess with the dogs. Who is this guy who dissed us, I want him found. His family, found. His friends, found. But not harmed and brought to me!"

One of the dogs spoke up. His name was Poodle. He had long

curly hair and very thin. His hand was also in a cast. He spoke in a very low laid-back voice.

"How are we suppose to bring this dude to you unharmed? He broke three hands, and Beagle is lying in his crib with his head beat in. We will have to kill this dude to get him here."

Doberman slammed his cast on the table and yelled, "This punk is mine! And only my wrath will be put on him. Drug him, tie him up, use handcuffs, I don't care. But bring him to me!" Doberman then jumped on the table and said, "Use all your police contacts and snitches to find this guy. Now go, go, go!"

Poodle pulled Doberman aside as the dogs left his pen. "Dog, this isn't going to be easy. That dude is crazy. Why don't you let this be? Let it go."

"We have sixty-six dogs. He is one man. We will take him down in time once we find him," Doberman said.

Poodle just shook his head and left his pen. As he left, the Doberman screamed at him, "Are you scared, Poodle!"

Poodle then slammed the door behind him and went to his car, a 1969 GTO Judge. It was in mint condition. He got it from a car collector who owed Poodle money. He then drove to see Beagle.

Poodle arrived at Beagle's crib. He walked through the door and into his bedroom.

"What's up, dog?" he said.

"Beagle answered, "What happened at the meeting?"

Poodle said, "He let the dogs out on the dude."

Beagle said, "The dude has it coming. For what he did to me and Doberman, you just can't diss him like that!"

Poodle looked at the beaten body of Beagle and said, "I've never seen fear in Doberman's eyes till that dude."

"You better keep a lid on that, dog. You talk like that around the Doberman, he will stick the big dog on you and beat you down." Beagle looked at Poodle. "You know that dude scared Doberman."

"I know, dog," Poodle replied, "that he's scared!"

A short while later, as Poodle left his crib, he said, "Take care, dog. I've got to start looking for this guy. Hopefully, he left town."

Poodle went downtown to see what he can find out about the dude. His first stop was a police officer. His name was Don Veal. He was about five feet eleven, a little overweight. He had a big nose, balding hair, and he talked out the left side of his mouth. He had given information to him several times. He was on the take. A dirty cop. He was sitting in his unmarked cop car at the park eating a doughnut.

Poodle walked up and said, "What's up, copper!"

The policeman said, "What's going down, man?"

Poodle answered, "I need some information on the dude who beat down on us. He was arrested. I need a name, where he stays, what kind of car he drives, and any relatives he might have here."

The cop held out his hand as Poodle dropped $300 in his hand. The cop said, "That will get me started. Just give me a couple of days." He threw his doughnut at the back of Poodle's car, laughing as he drove off.

Poodle shouted, "Screw you, BC."

BC was Veal's code name. It stood for baby cow. He drove off.

*****

At the construction site that Bryce was working, the foreman stopped by to see how Bryce was doing. Bryce was at the back finishing up. The foreman walked around the house, looked it over real good, and was amazed. He came up behind Bryce and said, "Looks real good. Real good, man. You're fast."

Bryce said, "How about the other two houses?"

The foreman said, "You can have them." He handed Bryce a check.

Bryce looked at it and said, "Good money."

Then the foreman said, "Bryce, have you got a place to stay?"

Bryce pointed at his truck and said, "Right there."

The foreman put his arm around him and said, "Let me help you a little." He pointed. "There is a work trailer over there. It's mine. You can sleep there. I got a bed in the back with AC and a small TV.

You can stay there till you get back on your feet." He then handed him a key.

Bryce took the key and said, "You're a good man."

The foreman said, "You are to just remember it's not the Plaza. It has a porta john beside it. Why don't you roll one of those barrels over here and fill it up with freshwater so you so you can at least clean up a little after work." He patted Bryce on the back. "I have to run."

As the foreman got in his truck and shut his door, his cell phone rang. It was Jamie.

She said, "Did he take it?"

"Yes," he replied. "He's a very good brick mason. I would keep him if he was sticking around."

Jamie said, "Maybe he will. Maybe he will."

"Your kinda sweet on him, aren't you, Jamie?"

She said, "Let's just say I owe him, so keep an eye on him for me."

He just said okay and hung up his phone.

*****

Bryce was rolling a barrel over to the trailer. He then grabbed the water hose and started filling the barrel. A few minutes later an unmarked police car pulled in. It was Officer Veal. He got out of his car off and walked up to Bryce.

He said, "Bryce? Bryce Hix?"

He answered, "Yes, that's me. Who wants to know?"

"We need an address for you or a place where you're staying and a phone number where we can reach you at."

Bryce just said, "Why?"

The officer snapped back, "We need more. I will take you back in right now!"

He felt a little funny about this cop, so he said, "I am staying at the cancer research center." He then gave him his cell phone number. He just made up a room number at the center.

The policeman then pointed at Bryce's truck and said, "Is that yours?"

JIM IVY

Bryce just nodded. The officer wrote the information down. He then asked Bryce while pointing his finger and circling his arm, "You're working in this housing addition for Nixon homes."

Bryce nodded his head again.

Officer Veal looked up and said, "I can't hear your head rattle!"

Bryce then answered yes, gritting his teeth.

The officer sat back in his car, closed the door to his car, then sped off. He drove back to the park and waited for Poodle to arrive. After fifteen minutes, Poodle drove up and parked right beside him. They both rolled down their windows.

Poodle said, "You have something for me."

The policeman pulled out a piece of paper and started to hand it to Poodle, but then he pulled it back and said, "You have something for me?"

He just rolled his eyes, then pulled out a wad of hundred dollar bills. He handed the officer three.

Then the officer gave him a piece of paper but then pulled it back and tossed it up into the air. The wind caught it and blew it into the pond.

Poodle yelled at him, "What the hell are you doing, man!"

Officer Veal answered, "Here is another one." He started to hand him another piece of paper. "If you want this one, it will cost you more."

Poodle then counted out more money and told him, "Choke on this!"

Veal handed him the piece of paper and said, "Nice doing business with you." He rolled up his window and sped off.

Poodle then took out his cell phone and called Doberman.

"Talk to me, dog," he said.

"I have that information you wanted. What now?"

"Check out the information. Make sure it's right up, and come back with the best time to catch this dead man. Then we will make a plan for him." Doberman then pounded his fist on the dash of his pimped-out Hummer. He shouted, "I got you. In a couple days, you're mine!"

Poodle then drove to one of his ladies' houses. He walked in the door. She ran up to him, hoping for an evening fix. She was reaching in his pocket. He grabbed her by the hand and said, "Bitch, do you have an alarm clock."

She pointed over toward the bed, on the nightstand.

Poodle told her, "Set it for 5:30 a.m. and make it loud." He pushed her toward the bed.

The young woman set the alarm clock. Poodle started getting undressed and held out a little baggie of crack and dangled it back and forth. The woman took off her clothes and crawled into bed. She started kissing all over his body. He grabbed her by the back of the head and shoved it toward his rock-hard penis. He said, "Do it right, girl, get a treat," as dangled the bag higher. He then lay on the bed as she pleasured him, and when he came, he said, "Good girl," and patted her on the head like she was a dog. Poodle told her, "Get me a towel. You better not let me oversleep," tossing the bag of crack toward the bathroom. She ran to the bathroom, grabbed a towel, then wiped him clean. She lay there at his until he said, "Okay, you can have it." She kissed him, hurried to the baggie on the floor, and went to the bathroom to have her fix. Poodle could hear her moaning with pleasure. She was good. She came back to bed and lay beside him in her crack dreamworld.

Five hours later the alarm came on blaring, waking Poodle. The young woman barely moved. Poodle got out of the bed and took a quick shower. While drying off, he came out of the bathroom. The young woman was lying on the bed naked as the day she was born. She was beautiful. As he looked at her, he felt himself getting hard so he grabbed her by the legs and pulled her to the end of the bed and gave it to her doggy style. When he was finished, he wiped himself clean and got dressed.

Poodle then drove to the cancer research center, parked in the parking lot where he could see the whole lot. He just waited about 6:30 a.m. when a black truck pulled in to the parking lot. The license plate said, "Brick Man." Poodle watched him get out of his truck. He then followed him into the hospital. He needed to see what kind of security there was. Poodle stayed at a distance. He watched Bryce get into the elevator and punch a button and go up. He watched the elevator to see where it stopped. It went directly to the twelfth floor. Poodle said to himself, "I got you now, bitch."

As Bryce was getting out of the elevator and walking toward his mother's room, he heard a voice calling out to him. It was Jamie. She came running up to him. Jamie was out of breath, and when she came up to him, he waited outside the door.

She said, "I need to talk to you, Bryce."

He looked away. He didn't want to be looking into those beautiful green eyes. He could not make or let Jaime know how he felt. So staring at the door of his mother's room, he answered sternly, "What do you want?"

She answered, "You have to listen to me. We have inside sources telling us the dogs are planning to kill you. It's all over the street. We have to protect you. Maybe you should stay at the police station in protective custody, or you could stay with a police officer just for your own protection."

He answered, "I am not hiding. Besides, I was going to stay with you but that didn't work out. Too much stress involved with your family. I have a place. No one knows where I'm at. I will be fine."

Suddenly, Jamie grabbed him by the arm. She spun him around. "You have to listen to me. This is not a game. It's serious. They kill people!" She then said, "Let me pick you up after work. Let's have dinner or drink. I have a safe place. We can go where you will be safe. We can talk and plan a strategy for the next few weeks."

Bryce just stood there. His knees were trembling with a touch of her hand on his arm. Without thinking, he said, "Okay, I'll be done about six. Meet me at the job site." He was looking off to space when he said that. Bryce paused before he pushed the door open. He wanted to say something, but his pride got the best of him. He pushed the door open and went in.

Jamie stood at the door as it closed behind her. Jamie then had a big sigh of relief because she knew the trouble he was in. She went back to the station to check in and follow up on a few leads.

GRIP

*****

Meanwhile, Bryce went over and hugged his mother and said, "How did the treatment go this morning?"

His mom tried to explain how tired she was from the treatment, but she asked how he was and if the job was going okay and if he was eating right. Like all moms she was worried about her son. After Bryce and his mother talked a little while, Bryce said he had to go. She understood. He left the room and hurried to the elevator. He jogged through the parking lot to his truck and suddenly stopped and stared at his truck. Someone had spray painted a message on the windshield. It said, "Your time is short, Brick Man." He then walked to the back of his truck. He then pulled his keys from his pants' pocket. He opened the back, reached in, pulled out a rag. He cleaned the words off his truck. He thought that maybe my mother is in danger, so he walked back into the treatment hospital and went to the security office to talk to someone about keeping an extra eye on his mother's room.

He knocked on the door.

An elderly gentleman named Ray said, "Come in."

He came in and sat down.

Ray said, "How can I help you?"

Bryce answered, "Are you the head of security?"

Ray said, "Yes."

"My mother is in room 1223. Will you keep extra watch of our room. There are some punks who want to hurt me, and I'm worried about her."

Ray then took all the information down that Bryce had. Then Bryce gave Ray his cell number and said, "Call me anytime."

The security guard said, "Don't worry, I will handle this."

Bryce then jumped back in his truck and sped back to his job site. He worked at a feverish pace. His helper could hardly keep the brick and mortar to him. They took a break at lunchtime.

Jose, the brick helper, told Bryce, "You are working too hard, I can't keep up."

Bryce just smiled at him and said, "We need to keep at this pace. I have to make a good showing today. Just hang in there, it's not going to kill you."

At five o'clock the house was nearly finished. Bryce could see his helper was worn out. The helper had worked very hard today. He told his helper he could take off now.

The helper replied, "Thanks. I'm very tired." He waved and walked to his car, opening the door and grabbing his two-gallon water thermos, pouring it over his head and then drinking it like he had been in the desert all day.

Bryce then went over to his trailer, pulled his shirt off, and turned the water hose on. He grabbed a bar of soap and gave himself a sponge bath outside. He then went inside, dried off, and changed his clothes. He then ran a brush through his hair and splashed on some cologne. He then sat down and tried to calm down. He was so nervous he could not sit still. His mind kept racing. *Is this a date, or is this just her job. Will I know after tonight?* He looked at his alarm clock. It was nearly six o'clock. He then started pacing inside the trailer.

The six o'clock whistle blew from a nearby glass plant. Bryce nearly jumped out of his skin. He looked out of the trailer window, and there she was. He took a deep breath. He opened the door and walked down the three steps to her car. Her door opened, and Bryce sat down inside her car.

"How are you?" Jaime said.

He replied, "Fine, how are you?"

They both sat there in silence, trying not to show any emotion.

He said, "Where are we going? I'm starved."

She said, "A place called Stans. The owner is one of my best friends. Her name is Kelly."

He sat there with a puzzled look on his face.

She then said, "It was her father's place. He passed away last year, so now the club and restaurant is hers. They have burgers and fries, sandwiches and chips, and salsa. Everything there is good."

He nodded his head.

They drove in silence for a few miles, then a parking lot appeared with a huge sign saying, "Stan's Place." In the parking lot was about thirty police cars.

He thought, *Great, more cops. No wonder she said we would be safe here.*

Jamie turned to Bryce and said, "This is a fun place. You can relax and feel safe." She smiled at him.

His heart sank. That smile of Jamie's had only lived in his heart for the past seventeen years.

As they walked into the restaurant, he couldn't help but notice there was only policeman inside. They walked over to a table and sat down. A very pretty lady walked up to Jamie and hugged her. It was Kelly. She gave Bryce the once over, looked him up and down, and said, "Nice to meet you."

He said, "Likewise, I'm sure."

Then Kelly said, "I have to get back to work. Are you going to sing later?"

Bryce looked puzzled and said, "Sing?"

Jamie said, "This is a karaoke bar and grill. You have to sing for your supper no matter how bad you are, and if you're the best of the night, your bill is on the house."

Kelly said, "Jamie and Randy baby win all the time. See you later?" She skipped across the floor and jumped back behind the bar.

Bryce sat back in his chair, folded his arms, and said, "I really don't have to sing, do I?"

Jamie said, "Maybe, just maybe."

A waitress then came over and took their order. Jamie reached her hands across the table toward Bryce. He quickly pulled them back. He couldn't hold her hands, but how could she understand that?

She pretended it didn't bother her. She looked at Bryce and said, "We have to protect you. The dogs are coming after you."

"I know," he said as he shrugged his shoulders. "They left a message on my truck."

Her eyes got big as watermelons and said, "You have to help me. You can't keep these things from me. Where and when did this happen?"

JIM IVY

"At the hospital," he said.

She then pulled her cell phone out and started to call.

Bryce said, "I already talked to the security office. They moved a security monitor to her room. They're going to monitor her a room 24/7, or I wouldn't be here right now."

She still tried to call her captain to provide some extra security.

Bryce said, "The security guard at the hospital took her name off the door as a precaution. So let's eat our meal and will stop by afterwards."

As Bryce and Jamie were eating their meal, the karaoke machine was turned on and the police officers started singing one at a time and the crowd was getting a little rowdy. Then the door opened, and in came Randy Bell and Officer Jones. The crowd opened up for them like they were rock stars.

Bryce said, "So what's the big deal about them?"

Jamie answered, "Well, Randy has won a free meal eleven nights in a row in the karaoke challenge. He has a real nice voice."

They walked right over to the table.

Randy said, "Hi, sis." He knelt down and gave her a big kiss on the cheek.

Bryce just nodded his head.

Randy said, "Are you going to sing tonight, Bryce? Or is that too scary for tough guys like you?"

Jamie spoke right up. "He doesn't have to!"

"I know," said Randy. "I was just kidding." He and Jones laughed and walked toward the stage.

Jones took the microphone, and he sang first. There was a mild cheering for him. Then Randy grabbed the microphone. The crowd started cheering for him before he even started singing. And after he sang a song you would have thought he was a star.

Then Kelly got on stage and said, "Any challengers, or does he get another free meal?"

Someone shouted from the back.

"I'll take that challenge."

It was Bryce.

The crowd suddenly was quiet as Bryce took the microphone and searched for a song. His eyes perked up when one of his favorites was there. He programmed it in and then sang his heart out to the crowd. The crowd cheered louder and louder for Bryce.

When Bryce was done, Randy jumped back on stage and said, "Wait a minute, wait a minute, let's do this one more time." So Randy chose another song. He sang even better this time and handed the microphone back to Bryce.

He took the mic again and said, "I beat you once. I don't have to do it again," and handed him the mic and walked off the stage! He walked back to Jamie's table and asked her if she was ready to leave.

She just smiled and said, "Okay."

As they were leaving, Randy was shouting at Bryce, "Get back here, get back here. Come on, come on!"

But Bryce and Jamie hurried out the door. The police crowd was all clapping for Bryce. Kelly walked up to Randy and said, "Face it, you lost. We knew this day was bound to happen someday." She then gave him a big hug. Kelly and Randy have been dating for about two years.

Randy snapped at Kelly, "You don't understand. I won't lose to him." He then slammed the microphone on the floor.

*****

Bryce and Jamie left in her car on the way to the hospital to see his mother. As they drove, the only sound you could hear was silence. Neither had much to say as she pulled into the parking lot and turned off her car. She put her keys in her purse and opened the door. She turned back toward Bryce. Their eyes locked on each other. Without thinking they let their emotions get the best of them. They grabbed each other and had a passionate kiss. Their hearts were pounding and rekindling the love they have for each other all out in one kiss.

As they pulled away, they both felt the barrels of cold steel against their heads. Then one young man said, "Don't move, lovers, or you're dead."

JIM IVY

Four young men with four guns were pointed at the two of them. One of them pulled Jamie's purse out and told Bryce to give him his wallet. He then pulled his driver's license out and read his name to himself. He said to the other three dogs, "This is him."

"What about her?" one of them said.

They looked through her purse and found her badge and cuffs.

"She's a cop. We will have to take her to the big dog. He will know what to do," one of the gang shouted.

One of them put the handcuffs on them. He put one cuff on Jamie. When he reached for Bryce's hand, Bryce grabbed the gang member's hand and crushed it with all his strength. Adrenaline was pumping through his veins, then he kicked the car door open, knocking two of the gang members to the ground. Jamie grabbed the other gang member's hand and shoved his gun toward the roof of her car. In the struggle, the gun went off twice. Bryce reached across Jamie, pulling the door handle, and shoved Jamie out the door, knocking the gunman to the ground.

Bryce and Jamie tumbled out the door onto the pavement. Bryce quickly kicked the gun out of his hand, and it slid under the car. The others were getting to their feet. Bryce grabbed Jamie by the belt and took off running low, snaking through the parking lot with gunshots firing at them. They ran toward a twelve-story office building. They reached the door. It was locked with a huge padlock on the door. Bryce grabbed it in both hands and let out a grunt. As he squeezed the lock, the lock popped open from the pressure of his grip. He pulled the chain off, and simultaneously, Jamie and Bryce kicked the door open. They went inside, frantically searching for the stairs.

Jamie yelled out, "Over here." She pushed open the door and waved at Bryce to come. They hit the stairs, running each floor. They tried the door. They were locked. Both were out of breath. They panted more and more with each floor they climbed. Finally, on the ninth floor Bryce stopped. He bent over, holding his knees, trying to catch his breath. Jamie stopped halfway up the stairs, leaning over the stairs. Looking down, she could see four or five young men racing up the stairs. They were barking, trying to scare Bryce and Jamie. Jamie motioned to Bryce, waving her hand and whispering, "Come on, don't stop. You can make it.

They continued up until they reached the top floor. They both heaved and kicked the door open. They were on the roof. They ran franticly to the edge of the building, looking for another way out. There was none. They looked at each other, as if to say, "What are we going to do now?" Bryce looked over the side, hoping to find a way. It was pitch dark.

On the west side of the building, a car drove through the alleyway. As Bryce looked over, he caught a glimpse of something in the flash of the light. He moved toward the image. He saw trying to line himself, motioning for Jamie to "Come here." As he started to point down, five dog gang members arrived on the roof with their guns raised and pointed at Bryce and Jamie.

As the dogs closed in, she slid behind him. He whispered to her, "Whatever happens I've got you. Don't worry."

One of them pointed the gun at Bryce. They were fifteen feet away, moving slowly toward Bryce and Jamie.

One of the dogs tapped him on the shoulder and said calmly, "You shoot the dude in the leg, and when he drops, I'll take her out."

The dog just nodded his head.

When he fired, Bryce pushed Jamie over the side. As they fell, Bryce grabbed her by the belt. They fell four stories. While falling, he reached down and grabbed a flagpole on the side of the building. The force of the fall was like a head-on collision. Jamie was knocked unconscious as she slammed into the side of the building. Bryce had locked onto the flagpole with one hand and held Jamie by her belt with the other.

The dogs were looking over the side. They couldn't see anything. The building was pitch dark on that side. They looked at each other. "Where did they go? They were all puzzled. All they could here were police sirens.

One of them said, "Let's get out of here!"

Police sirens were coming closer.

JIM IVY

One of the gang members said, "They have to be dead."

The dogs fled for the stairs as the police sirens were getting closer and closer.

Bryce was just hanging there, holding on to Jamie. He kept talking to Jamie. "Jamie, Jamie, you have to wake up."

From a distance Bryce could see the police lights flashing. An hour passed. It seemed like three. His only hope was for Jamie to wake up. Suddenly, she started moaning. Her eyes opened, and she screamed.

Bryce said, "Quit squirming around, like this it's hard enough without you wiggling around."

She looked up at Bryce and said, "My God, don't let go."

He chuckled. "No shit!" Bryce said, "Reach into my pocket and get my cell phone." He was talking barely above a whisper.

Jamie carefully reached into his pocket.

He said, "Don't drop it."

She sarcastically said, "No shit!" She dialed 911. She told the police dispatcher who she was and then told him to radio their location to the police cars at the cancer research center.

All the police were there in seconds even though it felt like hours to Bryce. Search lights were put on them. A fire truck came within minutes and pulled down the alleyway. The police officers on the scene called Officer Jones and Randy Bell. When they both arrived, they couldn't believe what they were seeing. Bryce was hanging from a flagpole, holding on to Jamie's belt as the ladder was being raised.

Jamie said, "Shit, Bryce, my belt is breaking or coming loose. Give me your hand."

Bryce said, "No, grab my hand, and hang on to it. If I grab yours, I'll break it." Then he thought, *Put the handcuffs onto my wrist.*

As she grabbed hold of his wrist, her belt snapped and her pants ripped but she locked the cuffs on to their wrist.

Bryce said, "Hang on, baby, hang on. Don't let go!" Bryce then grabbed her with his legs and locked them around her waist.

A fire truck ladder was being raised toward them. It was right under her feet. She could feel the ladder with her feet. A fireman reached out and grabbed her by the ankles.

He said, "I've got you." He told Bryce to let go.

He let go with his legs, but the handcuffs was holding her wrist together.

The firemen yelled down, "Send up a handcuffs key."

Jamie was now standing on the ladder. This had relieved some pressure off Bryce. She kept telling Bryce, "Hang on, they're coming."

He couldn't feel anything in his arm, but he didn't tell her that. The key was brought up and handed to Jamie. She unlocked the handcuffs. She was loose now. They tried to get her to go down, but she wouldn't till Bryce was safely on the ladder.

She told Bryce, "Let go, the ladder is right under you."

He said, "I can't. My hand is locked and can't feel anything."

They raised the platform. Finally, his feet was touching the platform. Jamie reached for his hand, trying to pry it off. She pulled and pulled on his fingers but could not get them off. Suddenly a cracking sound was heard. The flagpole was breaking loose from the building. The fireman reached up to Bryce and pulled on his fingers. The cracking sound was getting more and more intense. The pole snapped from the building, hitting Bryce in the head. Jamie and the firemen had caught Bryce on the ladder platform, but now he was unconscious and still hanging on to the flagpole. They lowered the ladder down with the flagpole dangling. Other firemen climbed up the ladder to help them hang on to Bryce and somehow secure the flagpole. They were all the way down to the ground now. They laid Bryce on the ground as three firemen pried his fingers from the flagpole with a crowbar. They had taped up the end, trying not to cut or damage his fingers. Carefully, they pried each finger until his hands were free.

One fireman said to the other, "I've never seen anything like that."

Randy and Officer Jones came running over. Randy put his hands out to help his sister up.

"Are you all right?" he said.

She said, "I'm fine, but Bryce is unconscious."

A small trickle of dried blood had run down the side of Jamie's face. She too had hit her head when she slammed into the wall a few hours ago.

Randy walked over to Bryce and grabbed him by his shirt. "What the hell did you do to my sister?"

Jamie yelled at Randy, "You don't know what the hell you're talking about." She quickly ran over to her brother and shoved him off Bryce and got right in his face, pointing her finger at him, while Randy moved backward, trying to avoid the finger shaking in his face. Jamie said, "He saved me. He saved my life. He kept me safe again. You don't have a clue, so keep your damn hands off of him!"

Randy looked puzzled. He didn't know what she meant by again.

Jamie then helped a fireman lift Bryce into the ambulance. She got in too and told the firemen, "Shut the fucking door!"

As the ambulance pulled away, Randy pounded his fist on the side of the ambulance.

Jamie's father Rock Bell pulled in as the ambulance was pulling out. He jumped out of his car, rushing over to the ambulance. As it left, he turned to Randy and said, "Is she all right? Is she hurt?"

Randy looked at his father and said, "Unfortunately, she is just fine. She is as stupid as ever."

His father got right in the face of Randy, pointing his finger at his face just like Jamie did and said, "You better start explaining yourself, boy. I'm still man enough to whip your ass!"

Randy pulled back, disgusted with the tone of the last two conversations he had with his sister and father. He sarcastically said, "All I know when I got here, Jamie was hanging from the flagpole." Randy pointed to the flagpole that was lying on the ground. "The fire department lifted the ladder up and brought both of them down." Randy then said with plenty of attitude, "That's the second time in the last five minutes someone has jumped in my face, and the next person that does it is going to get his ass kicked." Randy then told Officer Jones and his father, "Let's go to the hospital, and find out what's going on."

*****

Bryce and Jamie were admitted at the hospital emergency room. A couple of young doctors and nurses were checking them out. Bryce had to have fourteen stitches in his head, and Jamie had five. The doctor then bandaged Bryce's hand. He said to the other doctor, "But it looks like they pried his hand off of something, and his shoulder appears to be separated."

Bryce was still unconscious when they were finished with him, so they checked him in to a room. As the young doctor finished with Jamie, he questioned her about Bryce. He told her, "He should be fine. You can wait in the waiting room until he comes around."

The doctor had checked out Jamie thoroughly and told her what floor Bryce was on and the room number. Jamie walked out of the emergency room, went to the elevator, punched the button to floor 2. She found Bryce's room and peeked in.

A nurse spoke to her. "It will be a few minutes before you can see him. The waiting room is down the hall." She pointed to the left.

Jamie walked down the hall to the waiting room. She stopped at a vending machine, and then she remembered her purse was in her car. She had no money. Jamie sat down in the waiting room. She was rubbing her head when her father, brother, and Officer Jones came in.

Randy grabbed his father by the arm as Officer Jones sat down beside Jamie. Randy said to his father, "Do you know what she meant when she said he saved my life again?"

His father looks surprised, but instead of telling him, he just shrugged his shoulders and said, "You will have to find out from her."

Officer Jones asked Jamie, "What the hell happened tonight?"

She raised her head up, looking into the eyes of Officer Jones, and said, "Do you have a dollar? I need a Diet Coke." She pointed to the vending machine.

Officer Jones opened his wallet and pulled out a dollar and purchased the Diet Coke and gave it to Jamie.

She quickly opened it and took a drink. Jamie paused and said,

"It was the dogs. They tried to kill us as they chased us. We ended up on the roof of the building. They had us cornered. One of them started to shoot his gun. When he fired, Bryce pushed me over the side of the building. Somehow on the way down, he grabbed the flagpole. Don't ask me how he did it? He just did it. I hit my head on the side of the building from the jolt of the fall. He hung on to my belt. I don't remember how long. When I woke up, I was hanging there and he was holding on to me."

Officer Jones, with a puzzled look on his face, said, "How the hell could anyone fall from a twelve-story building and grab on to a flagpole, much less hang on to someone else?"

She said, "I don't know, but we had to pry his fingers off the flagpole. Just ask the firemen."

He then rubbed her head and said, "Are you okay?"

She said, "Yeah, fine! Randy just pissed me off!"

Randy stormed over to Jamie and said, "What did you mean by 'again'?"

Jamie told him what had happened some seventeen years ago before the wrestling match and how Bryce had saved her from possibly being raped or beat up or even killed.

Officer Jones said, "Well, you don't know that for sure."

She answered, "Those bullies were all convicted of rape some two months later. They had raped and beaten four other young girls." Her voice started cracking from the emotion. "Don't tell me I don't know!"

Officer Jones put his arm around her and hugged her as tears ran down her face. Her nose was running. She sniffed a few times. She whispered, "Don't let go."

As Officer Jones squeezed her tighter, things were becoming clear to him. Now he understands what this man means to her. Officer Jones held Jamie in silence for a few moments. As Randy started to say something, Officer Jones raised his hand and waved him back, a quiet way of telling him to shut up. Officer Jones pulled away from Jamie and said, "I have to go to the restroom." Getting up from the waiting room couch, he walked down the hallway but stopped and looked into the room Bryce was in. He walked in. A nurse was giving Bryce an IV.

He asked the nurse, "How is he doing? Is he going to be all right?"

She turned to him and said, "Yes, he will be fine. He just needs some fluids and some rest."

Officer Jones then walked up to Bryce and looked at him. He grabbed him by the face and said, "Can you hear me?" while shaking his face back and forth gently.

The nurse said "I doubt it. They gave him a pretty heavy dose to help him rest. He is out of it."

He then picked his hand up and squeezed it and said, "Thank you, thank you for saving Jamie. Maybe I was wrong about you." He then dropped his hand and walked out of the room and went straight to the waiting room.

Randy and his father were sitting next to Jamie. They both asked at the same time, "How is he?"

Officer Jones gave them the thumbs-up.

Jamie stood up and said, "I'm really tired. I just want to lie down. Can you take me home?"

Officer Jones said, "Sure."

Jamie's father gave her a big hug and said, "Go get some rest, baby."

Randy just nodded his head and said, "See you later, sis."

Jamie's father then told Officer Jones, "Bring her to my house. And I won't take no for an answer." He told Randy, "Come on, I will drop you off at the gym."

*****

Jamie's father pulled into the driveway as Officer Jones was helping her into the house. Jamie had lived here most of her life. He ran up the steps and opened the door for his daughter.

"This is going to be great, just like old times." He smiled.

Then Jamie said, "Crap! I need to call his mother so she won't worry, but I don't have my purse. Her number is in my cell phone."

Officer Jones said, "Stop! Don't worry about it. I will take care of it. I will stop by there before I go back to the police station."

CHAPTER 4

A New Dog Meeting

Halfway across town a meeting was being held at the dog pen. Poodle and four other dog were present. Doberman came up from the basement where he had been working out on his speed bag. Sweat was rolling off his face. He unwrapped his cast hand and then glared at Poodle. In a somber voice, he then asked Poodle what happened.

"How is this guy not in my basement or at my boat, or maybe you should just show me one of his hands that you had to cut off because you had to kill him."

Poodle rolled his eyes, then said, "All I know the dogs had the dude cornered on the roof. He has taken up with a lady cop. They took a shot at one of them, and the dude jumped off the roof and took her with him. It was twelve-stories high. They thought he was dead. He had to be dead."

Doberman said, "Dead, dead. Didn't they try and pick them up with the spatula! And bring him to me."

Poodle replied, "Listen, dog, when they got downstairs, the police was everywhere. So they had to split."

Doberman asked, "How could anyone jump off of twelve-story building and be okay?"

Poodle answered, "He grabbed on to a flagpole."

"A flagpole? How do you grab a flagpole falling from the top floor and then hang on not only to himself but his girlfriend too." He stared down at Poodle, waiting for an answer.

Then Poodle stood up well to Doberman and said, "This is a bad, dude. Why don't we let this one go, dog?"

Doberman then pushed Poodle against the wall and said, "Maybe we need to change our tactics. We're going at this all wrong. We will make him come to us. Find out who the bitch cop is and how we can get to his mom. That's what we will do." He then looked back at Poodle. "Can you handle that, dog? Or do I have to get Bulldog to do it?" he said sarcastically.

Poodle walked outside to his car and leaned against it. He pulled his cell phone out and called Officer Veal for some more information. Poodle told Veal what he needed and he would catch him later. Poodle sat down in his car. He rolled himself a Doobie and fired it up, thinking, *Someone is going to get killed. How many dogs will die for Doberman's vengeance.* He then started his car and pulled out and sped off.

*****

Officer Jones arrived back at the police precinct, sat down at his desk, then rubbed his hand. There was still pain in the hand from the grip of Bryce. His phone rang. It was his captain. He told him to get in his office.

Jones walked over to his office, walked into the door, and said, "What's up, Captain?"

"Sit down. How's the hand," he asked.

Jones said, "It's better."

The captain paused and looked at Officer Jones and said, "I just got a call from Jamie. Is she okay? She seemed very unreasonable on the phone. She wanted me to put some protection on the guy who put the squeeze on you and his mother. Does this seem rational to you? Or is she just shook up from whatever happened. I haven't seen the report yet, so maybe you can enlighten me."

Jones crossed his arms, took a deep breath, and said, "Well. it's like this. Jamie and Bryce Hix, the guy who nearly broke my hand, were hanging twelve stories in the air. The dogs took a couple of shots at them. She had a bump on the head, and Bryce probably saved her life, and all my sources say that the dogs will not stop till he is dead."

The captain sat back in his chair and tapped his pen on the desk several times and said, "Well, what do you think? Should we protect them?"

Officer Jones stood up and said, "Yes, protect him," and started out the door.

But the captain said, "Hold it right there. I'm not finished with you."

Jones stood in the doorway with his hand on the door.

"You haven't changed your mind about this Bryce Guy, have you? We have to prosecute him. We can't let people assault police officers. There has to be a punishment. We can't let this go. What kind of message are we sending to this city if we let him go? You are on board, right? Right?"

Then Jones raised his voice and said, "Can I go now?"

The captain answered back, "You can leave. And, Jones, send a couple of uniforms to protect this guy and his mother. She's a cancer patient, isn't she?"

Jones nodded his head.

"That's all we need, for her to get hurt while we were trying to prosecute her son."

Jones then pulled the door behind him and walked back to his desk and sat down. He picked up the phone and placed a call downstairs.

Officer Veal answered.

Jones told him to send a couple of uniform officers over to the cancer center. He said, "They are to call me on my cell phone, and I will fill them in who they are to protect." He sat back in his chair and thought, rubbing his head like he had a migraine headache. He stared at a picture of Jamie and Randy and himself. Those were good times. He thought, *Maybe I should call her and see how she is, or maybe not. What to do? What to do?* He kept saying over and over again in his mind, so then he picked up the phone and called Rock's house. It rang several times, then Jamie picked up the phone.

"Hello," she said.

"Hey, it's Jones. Were you resting?"

Jamie sighed and said, "No, trying to clean up some of this junk my father never cleans up a thing around here. Since Mom died, this house is a pigsty. Mom would have a cow if she saw the house like this."

Officer Jones said, "You should be resting, after all you have a week off. So get some rest, and I'll see you later."

Jaime hung up the phone and then called the hospital to check on Bryce. She talked to the nurse.

The nurse said, "He is a lot better and would be released tomorrow. His shoulder is a lot better."

Jaime felt better that she needed to keep busy, so she started cleaning the house. She decided to put some of the boxes of clothes in the attic. She pulled down the ladder and climbed up the ladder with a box in one hand and a flashlight in the other. As she was putting the box down, she tripped over an orange extension cord and fell on a box. The box broke open. Some old videotapes fell out and the old video camera she had used to tape Randy's wrestling matches. She started looking through them, then she wondered if the wrestling match between Bryce and Randy was in here. She sifted through the tapes. There must have been twenty or thirty tapes. Finally, she thought she had found it. It was marked number 19. Somewhere back in her mind she thought this was it. She hurried down the ladder and into the living room. She turned the TV on and the VCR and put the tape in. She was fast-forwarding through the tape till she could find the match. It seemed like hours, but it is only a few minutes. Finally, she found it.

Her eyes were glued to the TV. The match went back and forth. It was very close too. Bryce took Randy down and took control in the final minute. He was leading by the score of seven to five. Randy took a desperate chance to break free, but the referee walked right in front of the camera. She couldn't see what happened. Time expired. Randy was rolling on the mat in pain, holding his hand. It was broken. The referee had held up Bryce's hand and declared him the winner. Her father was yelling at the referee and the other coach. She couldn't hear what he was saying, but he was furious. He helped Randy up, and the team doctor took Randy away. Her father was sitting in his chair with a water bottle in his hand. He pulled out a bottle of pills and took one, then it looked like he was reading the bottle of pills.

Jamie had never seen this before. What was he doing?

He then looked around and drop several pills in the bottle and shook it up. Looking around, he tore the label off the water bottle. He then walked over to Bryce, stuck at his hand, and shook it. Then it did seem like her father was pointing his finger at Bryce. He was very angry, she could tell. Then he stumbled over a chair and dropped the bottle. It fell into a few other water bottles. Bryce and his coach helped her father up to his feet. He then pushed them away. Her father picked up a water bottle and walked away. Bryce then picked up a water bottle lying on the ground and drank it down till it was gone, then he picked up another one and started drinking it. He sat down, and it seemed he was looking in the crowd for someone. A person walked behind Bryce. She couldn't make out who it was because Bryce was blocking her view. He picked up the empty bottle Bryce had just drank, examined the label, and laid down another empty bottle. The man turned around. It was Jamie's father. He looked around and then left with the empty bottle in his hand. Jamie's jaw dropped.

"What did he do? My dad, my dad!" she exclaimed. She just shook her head. "He did it. He drugged Bryce."

She quickly pulled the tape out of the VCR, put it in her purse and turned the TV off. She started for the door but dropped her purse. Then she tripped over it, falling to the floor. She lay there for a few seconds, trying to calm down. She rolled over and gently got to her feet. She bent down picked up her purse, opened it, grabbed her car keys, and calmly walked out the door to her car. She started it and looked at the clock. It said 10:44 a.m. She was thinking her father would be at the gym. She needed to see him now.

She kept thinking in the drive over, how could her dad do this? He ruined Bryce's life. No gold medal. No wonder he was bitter. His life could have been so much different. The shame he had to deal with because no one believed him that he was innocent. She pulled into the parking lot. She was fighting back the tears of her anger, trying to remain strong. She walked into the gym, right over to her father who is getting a drink of water out of the fountain. She tapped him on the shoulder.

He turned and said, "Hey, baby, how are you feeling?"

She answered, "I know, Dad. I know what you did." She repeated it, waving the tape in his face. "I know what you did." She could see in his facial expressions that he knew what she was talking about, but he pretended not to. He would not even look into her eyes. "You switched water bottles with Bryce. What was in the bottle you gave him?"

"Who told you these lies? Him?" Rock said smugly.

"No one. I've seen it myself. It's all on the videotape! Does Randy know about this too?" she asked her father, who spun her around by the arm, pulled her into his office, and shut the door behind him.

"Now look, your brother has nothing to do with this. He doesn't know a thing. Now, kid, I've made a few mistakes in my life. But at the time I felt it was the right move. He cheated. He broke Randy's hand. As Randy was about to escape, the match would have been tied and went into overtime, but he cheated and broke his hand! I wasn't going to let fifteen years of training go down the drain by some punk sixteen-year-old kid. Your brother had never lost a match, and this kid was not going to waltz in and steal our gold medal," he said angrily.

Jamie lashed back and said, "Our gold medal? I didn't see you out there. It was Randy's blood and guts—"

He interrupted her. "Randy's blood and guts? What about all the time I put in with your brother? I pushed and molded him to perfection. He was unbeatable until that son of a bitch came along and tried to ruin things."

She shouted back at him, "What did you put in his drink?"

He glared at her and said, "Just a few steroids. My doctor had prescribed them for me. I never really thought they would come in handy, I didn't even think it would work. I grasped at a straw and pulled out a rose. They tested him, and steroids showed up in his system. They disqualified him, so your brother was named to the Olympic team and won the gold medal. Was it worth it? That's what you want to know, isn't it?"

She answered, "Yes, was it worth it destroying someone else's life."

He replied, "Yes, I do it again for your brother."

Jamie stared at her father. Tears were rolling down her face. "So Randy doesn't know."

He said, "No, he doesn't. I never told him, and you can't tell him. It would kill him. What, you want to hurt your brother? It's done. We can't go back. Now leave it alone. Just let it go, please, I am begging you!"

Randy had walked up to his father's office, knocked on the door, and came in. Both Jamie and her father stared right through him and didn't say a word.

Randy said, "Jamie, are you feeling better? You look awful, and why are you crying?"

She said, "I just had to talk to Dad about something. I have to go." She got up and walked over to her brother. She gave him a kiss on the cheek and started out the door.

Randy said, "What's your hurry? Stay, let's have lunch?"

She kept walking and went out to her car.

Randy turned his father and said, "What's her hurry? What did she want anyway?"

His father turned to Randy and said, "Nothing. It doesn't concern you."

"I'll bet it's that damn Bryce. I hope you told her he is no good.

Lord knows I have tried. She won't listen to me when it comes to him."

Rock walked over to Randy, put his arm around him, and said, "Son, sometimes we do things, even the wrong things, for love. What might be wrong to you could be blinded by love, and they could regret it the rest of their life." Then he walked off.

Randy, *What the hell does that mean? I must take after Mother because Jamie and Dad are idiots.*

*****

The next morning Bryce had checkout of the hospital early and went back to work. He had lost a day at half. When the taxi dropped Bryce off at the CRC, he noticed a police car in the parking lot patrolling slowly, and when he went inside, he noticed more security officers walking around, showing a presence. One of the security officers was Dallas. He was huge about six feet four with a deep voice.

Dallas asked Bryce if he could help him.

Bryce replied, "I'm just going up to my mother's room." Bryce told him the room number.

Dallas answered, "What's your name?"

"My name is Bryce Hix."

The officer stepped over to Bryce and said, "Let me take you up there." He pointed toward the elevator.

They both got on. Dallas pushed the button and stood quietly till it reached the floor. The door opened. Bryce stepped out and walked to his mother's room while Dallas stood outside the door. Bryce walked over to his mother's bedside. She was sleeping. He kissed on the head and sat down for a moment. Her eyes opened ever so slightly.

She whispered, "Bryce, is that you?"

He responded yes as he stood up so she could see him.

She asked, "Are you okay?"

He said yes with a smile. Bryce had hidden the bandage on his head under his baseball cap. Amy told him the treatment was wiping her out and she can't remember what day it is. Even though Bryce was concerned, he was really a little relieved. She would just worry about him if she knew everything that had happened the last couple of days. Bryce kissed her again, telling her he was late for work and he had to run.

*****

Bryce knew he had to work late to make up for the days he lost. He put up some work lights so he can work through the night.

As he was working, Jamie pulled in. She came running up to him and said, "Where have you been? I was worried. I'd tried and tried to phone. You wouldn't answer. I went to see your mom. She told me you are here."

Bryce looked at her and said, "You had my phone last, not me. I was just hanging around."

As he chuckled, Jamie then remembered she had the phone. It must be in her purse or at home or in her car. She opened her car, looked through her purse, and there was the phone next to the videotape.

Bryce said, "What's that?

She quickly pushed it aside and said, "It is your phone, but it looks like the batteries are dead."

He said, "Well, it hadn't been charged in a few days." So Bryce took the phone and plugged it into his charger in his truck. He turned back around and bumped right into Jamie.

She reached out and grabbed him around the waist. She looked into his eyes with quivering lips. She said, "Just kiss me."

He didn't hesitate. The kiss was very passionate. A single tear ran down Jamie's face. It dripped onto the face of Bryce.

He stopped and pulled away and said, "What's wrong? Why are you crying?"

She looked at him and just said, "Pain, I feel so much pain I have caused. You will never know how much."

JIM IVY

Bryce was puzzled. He said, "I feel nothing but joy and happiness when I'm with you."

"Just hold me," she said. "Please don't let me go, please!"

They embraced again, but Bryce felt there was something she wasn't telling him. He pulled back again and said, "Sorry, I have to get back to work. I have to finish this house tonight, and you're too much of a distraction to me. As much as I want you to stay, I have to finish, Jamie."

She said, "I can help!"

"I don't know, can you?"

She quickly answered, "I'm very strong. I can handle myself."

"Okay," he's said. "Then fill that bucket with the brick mortar, and bring it to me."

She took it as a challenge. Now she picked up the shovel, filled the five-gallon bucket. She picked it up with both hands, walking awkwardly, and carried it to Bryce. A full bucket of mortar weighs about eighty pounds.

"Where you want it?" she said.

Bryce answered, "Pour it on my mud board. There's some gloves lying over by the mixer, and it's easier if you carry two buckets at a time. It will even you out when you're carrying it."

They worked through the night. Three hours later Jamie sat down in Bryce's truck with the door open. She reached inside Bryce's ice chest and grabbed a bottle of water and started drinking it. She needed a break. She never realized how hard of work this was. Bryce had told her to take a break when she sat down. The next thing she knew she was waking up inside Bryce's truck. She had been asleep for about two hours. Bryce was cleaning his tools.

Jamie asked, "Are we done?"

He said, "Yes, let's get some breakfast."

They went to a local waffle house, and after they had ordered, Jamie told Bryce, "You know what today is?"

He shrugged his shoulders.

She said, "Today you go to court to find out if you're going to be charged."

He said, "Yeah, I know it doesn't look good for me. Your partner was pretty pissed off about his hand, and him being a good friend of your brother, that's another strike against me. I can't win for losing."

They just sat there and ate quietly, and when they were done, Bryce said, "How about I take you home so we can get cleaned up for the preliminary hearing. I'd like to take a shower in case they put me in for a while."

Jamie's teeth were grinding. She was saying a little prayer to herself and hoping Officer Jones would change his mind. In about three hours they would know.

CHAPTER 5

They arrived at Jamie's house, walking in together.

Jamie said to Bryce, "You take a quick shower, and then I will." She pointed toward the bathroom.

Bryce took his clean clothes with him, hanging them on the hook behind the door. Jamie handed him a towel, and he shut the door behind her. Jamie had gone to her closet and laid out the clothes she was going to wear. Jamie sat down at her dressing table, looking in the mirror.

"Oh my god!" she said to herself. She had mortar on her face and in her hair. She was filthy. As she sat there looking at herself, she thought, *He never said a word about how I looked!*

When Bryce was done, Jamie was in her robe. She had washed her face with her makeup removal wipes and brushed the mortar out of her hair. As Bryce came out, she zipped by him like the flash, shutting the door. Bryce was dressed and very tired. He sat down in her living room chair. He dozed off in seconds.

After showering, Jamie peeked out of the bathroom. She didn't see Bryce. In her robe, she walked over to her bedroom door and looked out into the living room. She saw Bryce asleep in the chair, so she quietly closed the door.

Forty-five minutes later, Jamie was dressed and ready. After one last look in the mirror, she woke Bryce up, telling him they needed to go. It was ten o'clock Monday morning. It was court day for Bryce.

*****

The district attorney was going over his notes, waiting for the judge to come in. Bryce was sitting at the other table, talking to his court-appointed attorney. Jamie was sitting in the row behind, listening.

In walked Jamie's partner, Officer Jones. He paused, then walked over to the district attorney and said, "Can I talk to you outside?"

They walked outside of the courtroom.

Jamie looked at Bryce and shrugged her shoulders as if to say, "What's that all about?"

Outside the courtroom Officer Jones looked into the district attorney's face and said, "I'm dropping the charges. I can't do it."

The attorney shouted at him and put his finger on his chest. "You're not dropping anything. We have to do this. He assaulted a police officer. This is not a traffic ticket!"

Jones grabbed the attorney's finger and said, "Stick that up your ass, or I'll do it for you! This guy saved my partner's life. I'm not sending him to jail. You can't make me testify against him. I will lie on the stand. Just drop the damn charges."

He replied back, "I am not dropping anything. You will testify, or I will hold you in contempt of court. You will be the one sitting in jail."

Officer Jones glared at him, and under his breath, he said, "Maybe your wife would like to know about those long lunches you take at the Top Hat Motel with that stripper every Thursday?"

The veteran attorney just shook his head and told Jones to, "Eat shit. I don't know why I bother trying to convict anybody." He pushed Officer Jones out of the way and walked back into the courtroom. He started putting his papers away into his briefcase and slammed it shut.

The judge came in.

The bailiff said, "All rise."

The judge started banging his gavel and said, "We are here regarding—"

The DA spoke up, interrupting the judge. "May I approach the bench." He walked up to the bench and told the judge, "We had to drop the case for lack of evidence."

The judge was listening to the district attorney, frowning the whole time, shaking his head. He then pointed his finger at the attorney and said, "This is not acceptable. Sit down." The judge then banged his gavel twice, cleared his throat, and said, "Case dismissed. Mr. Hix, you're free to go."

The bailiff told everyone to rise. The judge walked out of the courtroom, opened the door to the judge's chambers, and slammed it behind him.

Bryce turned to Jamie and said, "What the hell happened?"

She then hugged him across the table and said, "I'll see you later at the cancer center." She left the courtroom and ran down the hall.

Officer Jones was sitting in a coffee break room drinking a cup of coffee. Jamie walked in and sat down beside him and said, "Thank you."

Officer Jones said, "He can't be all bad. He saved your life twice. There are still some things in his past I don't like or feel comfortable with, like the girl he assaulted. But if he lays one finger on you, I will kill him. That's a fact!"

Jamie then hugged her partner of seven years because she knew he was in love with her for the past three years. She just didn't feel the same.

In walked Randy with a puzzled look on his face. He was shrugging his shoulders with his hands held out, palms up.

"Did I miss it? Is Hix already in jail? What happened?" he said. Randy looked at the both of them. "Shit, he walked, didn't he? Officer Jones, what the hell did you say? This was open and shut. How could he walk?" Randy looked puzzled.

Jamie smiled and shrugged her shoulders.

Randy grabbed Officer Jones by the shirt collar and said, "She got to you, didn't she? All she had to do was wiggle her ass, bat her eyes, and you caved in, you chicken shit. Why do you carry a torch for someone who don't love you, man? You are stupid. Why didn't you do the right thing!"

Officer Jones stood up, pushed Randy against the wall, and shouted at him, "I did the right thing." He then stormed out of the coffee break room.

Randy then turned with raised eyebrows and a scowl on his face to Jamie and said, "How could you do that? Officer Jones would do anything for you?"

Jamie responded, "I never asked him to do anything for me. Officer Jones is just not walking around with blinders on like you. He sees Bryce for what he is—a good and decent person who has had a few bad breaks in his life."

Randy clapped his hands together and shook them at Jamie and said, "A few bad breaks? Let's see, he took drugs, cheated to beat me, and blamed someone else. He assaulted a young woman, spent a little time in jail for that, and when he was a child, the police think he had killed his father but couldn't prove it."

Jamie glared at Randy, shook her head, and started waving her arms. "If you only knew the truth about Bryce, you would think differently."

As she started to tell him, her father stepped into the room and shouted at Jamie to "Shut up."

Jamie said, "Maybe we should tell him the truth."

Her father gently took her by the arm and escorted her out of the break room, talking under his breath, saying to her, "What are you doing? I can't tell him. He'll hate me and throw everything he has worked for away. What about the wrestling school he teaches, all those kids he has worked with? All the good Randy has done would be for nothing, so shut your pie hole and think of the big picture for once instead of yourself."

Jamie snapped back, "I'm not thinking of myself. What about Bryce? You screwed him up. What about him?"

Randy stormed out of the coffee shop. He could see his father and sister arguing down the hall, so Randy went the opposite way and walked around the corner and bumped into Bryce. Randy pushed Bryce away, pointed his finger in Bryce's face, and shouted, "Bryce, stay away from my sister!"

Bryce replied calmly, "Don't you think that's her choice?"

"No, it's not because I'm going to kick the crap out of you if you don't," Randy said.

"You might try, but I don't see it happening," Bryce said with a big smile on his face.

They were standing nose to nose when four police officers came over. One of the officers stepped between Bryce and Randy. You could cut the tension with a knife.

Officer Jenkins said, "Randy, you better chill out or we are going to escort you out of the building."

Randy turned to Bryce and said, "Would you like to go outside?"

Bryce said, "Sure."

Officer Jones came out of the bathroom. He had been listening at the door. He pointed to Officer Jenkins and said, "Take Randy out of here now!"

Officer Jenkins and one of the other officers escorted Randy out of the building.

Officer Jones pointed at Bryce. "Let's have a cup of coffee."

Randy shouted at Bryce as he left, "This isn't over!"

Bryce and Officer Jones went into the coffee break room. The other two police officers followed. Officer Jones told Bryce to have a seat.

"Would you like a cup of coffee or a Coke?"

Bryce nodded and said, "A Coke."

Officer Jones walked to the Coke machine, put some money in, and a Coke can came tumbling down. He then put some money in the coffee machine and got him a cup of coffee. He sat down across from Bryce and stared at him while drinking his coffee.

Bryce opened his can of Coke and took a sip. Bryce said, "Why are you protecting him? Why didn't you let him go outside with me? It would have been over by now. I would have kicked his ass all over the pavement."

Officer Jones answered, "He is my friend. I look out for my friends like Jamie. She would've been hurt to see you guys fighting.

You remember that. So you stay away from him, or you will answer to me."

Bryce just smiled at him.

"You're a cocky little bastard. The next time I'll use my nightstick or my .357 Magnum. Let's see you grip out of that," Officer Jones said.

Bryce said, "Can I go now?"

"Yes, but go out the back way," Jones said.

As Bryce was leaving the building and walking to his truck, he thought, *Maybe he was right. I should stay away from Jamie's brother for Jamie's sake. It would hurt her. She would have to choose, and I might lose if I'd make her do that. Maybe I should just end it. It would be better for everyone. Besides, she would just get hurt or I will. But will I ever get a chance at love with someone if not her? I don't think it will ever happen. Don't I deserve a chance?*

He drove to the cancer center to see his mother.

Maybe my mother will know what to do.

He pulled into the cancer center parking lot, walked inside, and stopped at the security office to see if any strangers had come by. As Bryce knocked on the door, the security officer shouted, "Come in." Bryce opened the door and stepped inside.

The officer was staring at all the security monitors. He turned and said, "Can I help you, sir?"

Bryce asked, "Has any strangers visited my mother since the last time I was here?"

The officer pulled out a clipboard that had a sign-in sheet on it. The officer had a logged entry for every visitor his mother has had. The officer studied the log for a few seconds and said, "No, your mother hasn't seen anyone she hasn't seen before," pointing to the names on the log sheet. He then smiled at Bryce, shaking his head side to side, pointing at the security monitors. He leaned back in his chair and said, "Your mother is safe with all the officers, security, and nurses around. She's safe, believe me."

Bryce said, "Thanks," patted him on the back, and went to her room. The elevator opened on his mom's floor. He was met by another security officer and a nurse. The officer stepped in front of Bryce. The officer was huge. He stood six feet four and had to weigh nearly three hundred pounds. His name tag on his uniform said "Dallas."

The nurse said, "He's okay. That his mom's room."

The security officer sat down and unfolded his newspaper, and the nurse smiled at Bryce, walking quickly to the next room. Bryce felt better that his mom was secure and safe. He opened the door. His mom was sitting in her chair with her Bible lying on her lap. She was asleep. Bryce stared at his mom for a moment. He noticed some hair lying on the floor. She looked so frail. He gently kissed her head and said, "Mom, it's your son."

She opened her eyes and smiled. She then said, "Well, you're here, so tell me what happened?"

He answered, "They dropped the case."

She said, "It's about time they got their stuff together."

Bryce interrupted her and said, "But how are you doing, Mom?"

Mrs. Hix took a deep sigh and said, "I'm weak from the chemo. My hair is starting to fall out, but I'm going to beat it, son." She gave her son a confident stern look.

Bryce said in a jest, "You're a tough old broad, aren't you, Mom?"

"The toughest," she said. "So what's new with the lady cop Jamie?"

"I'm glad you asked." He then went over every scenario he could think of.

His mom just sat there listening to her son as his voice cracked a few times. She could see it in his face and his body language. He was hurting with this one. It was obvious to his mom that Bryce was in love, maybe for the first time. He then unfolded his hands and buried his face in them.

She patted his head and said, "You have to follow your heart on this one. If you really care for her, don't let her get away. I have a good feeling about her. Don't think you don't deserve love. Everyone gets a chance at love. You just have to be brave enough to take a chance on it. You deserve love, my son."

He nodded his head and hugged his mom.

There was a knock on the door. It was Jamie.

His mom said, "Speak of the devil."

Jamie looked puzzled and said, "Were you talking about me?" She walked over and stood next to Bryce.

"No," said Bryce.

"Yeah, right," she replied jokingly, poking Bryce with her finger.

Bryce dragged another chair over for Jamie to sit down. They both sat there and visited with his mother. It seemed like hours. Mrs. Hix couldn't help but notice the chemistry between Bryce and Jamie and the way they looked at each other.

Mrs. Hix started to tear up when the nurse came in and said, "It's dinnertime, and we need to check some things. You will have to leave, so come back in about an hour."

Mrs. Hix said, "This is my nurse, Fernanda."

Fernanda was Hispanic, about five feet two, and had a beautiful smile. Fernanda shook the hand of Jamie and just patted Bryce on the shoulder. They both hugged and kissed her.

Jamie asked Bryce, "Are you hungry? Let's get something to eat."

He looked at his mother.

She said, "Go on, eat something and get some rest. I'll see you in the morning."

He nodded his head and left the room.

Mrs. Hix said to Fernanda, "I think my son loves Jamie." A single tear rolled down her face.

Fernanda replied, "I think you're right, just the way he looks at her." She then patted Mrs. Hix on her shoulder. "Let's take these pills and eat some food."

*****

Bryce and Jamie walked to his truck. He said, "Where are we going?"

Jamie replied, "How about the police bar and grill?"

Bryce wrinkled his nose, shaking his head no. "How about we go somewhere a little more private?"

JIM IVY

Jamie quickly answered, "How 'bout we go to my place and order a pizza?"

Bryce's eyes opened wide and said, "That sounds great." He then got in his truck.

She got in her car, and he followed her to her place. They arrived at her place. Neither said a word walking up to the door, but he wondered what would happen after the pizza. When they went inside, he asked, "Can I use the restroom?"

She pointed at a door down the hall.

He went into the restroom, then stared at himself in the mirror, thinking, *I can't do this. What if I hurt her? I couldn't forgive myself. I just got to get out of here somehow without hurting her feelings.*

Bryce came out of the restroom. Before he could say a word, she said, "The pizza is on its way. Do you want to watch TV or a movie or listen to music?"

Without thinking, he said, "Your choice."

She walked over to her CD player, turned it on, and the music started playing.

"I hope you like this," she said.

The music started playing. It was Elvis.

He just smiled and said, "He's the best."

They sat there listening to music and gazing into each other's eyes. Their hearts were pounding. He started to speak. The doorbell rang, and it was the pizza guy.

"Wow, that was fast," Jamie said. She then jumped up, grabbed her wallet out of her purse, and opened the door.

Bryce shouted, "Wait, I'll pay."

"Forget about it." She waved her hand at Bryce.

The pizza guy said, "Hey, Jamie."

She replied, "Hey, Mario," and paid him.

He then said, "See you next time."

Jamie took the pizza in the kitchen. She was getting plates down from the cabinet when she shouted to Bryce, "I have wine, beer, or Diet Coke to drink."

Bryce said, "Beer's fine."

Jamie shouted back, "Sit down, I'll bring it to you."

This was totally out of character for Jamie. She never waited on a man before, but it was something she wanted to do for Bryce.

They sat on the couch and ate their pizza while Bryce drank his beer and Jamie sipped on wine. They talked about meaningless things for about an hour. They both danced around the issue at hand. Was this going any farther tonight?

Bryce stood up and said, "Maybe I better go."

Jamie stood up and said, "Why not stay with me tonight?"

Bryce knew this might happen. He was torn. He didn't know what to say or do. He just stood there. Finally, she took Bryce by the hand. She looked deep into his eyes. A small tear trickled down her face.

Bryce's heart was melting. His voice quivered when he said, "I can't touch you. I might hurt you, and I would never forgive myself for that."

She nodded her head and said, "Let me worry about that." She led him to the bedroom and sat him down on the bed. She gave him a heart-stopping kiss.

His will was gone. He was giving in to the temptation.

Then she said, "I'll be right back. Make yourself comfortable." She went into the bathroom.

He thought, *I need to get out of here.*

As he started to get up, she came out in a see-through nightgown. His eyes were now locked on her. She was beautiful, perfect in every way. She walked slowly over to him. He thought he was going to explode before she even touched him. She started taking his shirt off, kissing each button, before removing it very slowly, one at a time. She then did the same to his jeans, kissing each button again. This was the most erotic thing to ever happened to him. She then gently pushed him back onto the bed. She laid him down. His hands were reaching for her, he then pulled them back. He was afraid. She reached into her nightstand and pulled out her handcuffs and twirled them around her finger several times. While smiling playfully, she then took his hand and wrist, placed the handcuffs on him, and hooked his hands to the bedpost one at a time. Her breasts rubbed across his face as she was doing it. She then pulled her nightgown slowly over her head. She then rubbed her breasts all over Bryce's mouth, exciting him and herself. She was moaning with pleasure. Then she laid her body on top of him and gently inserted his penis into her.

The love they were making was so beautiful there wasn't anything dirty about it. The passion went on and on until they both had used all the energy they had. They were so exhausted. She took the handcuffs off. She kissed him again and laid her head gently on his chest before falling asleep.

His last thought was, *I love this woman.* He then whispered, "I love you, Jamie. I've always loved you from the first time I laid eyes on you."

She smiled to herself, pretending to be asleep because she knew she wasn't meant to hear that.

They both fell asleep.

*****

Jamie's alarm rang at six thirty in the morning. Shaking Bryce gently, she whispered in his ear, "I love you too. Stay with me always. I have been waiting for you since the first day we met. You're the reason I wanted to be a cop. The way you took control and got me out safely, I could never forget that."

As she whispered, she noticed the corner of his mouth moving up. A smile came over his face. She then started tickling him. They rolled around on the bed, laughing.

Then she said, "You're not asleep you big faker." She got out of bed and headed for the bathroom. She stopped in the doorway. Her naked body leaned against the door frame. She turned toward Bryce and asked him, "What would you like for breakfast?"

Looking at her, she was so beautiful. With the sunlight barely coming through the mini blinds, he couldn't help but stare. Seconds later, his cell phone rang. It was the homebuilder. Bryce answered.

Jamie seductively whispered to him, "Are you kidding? Look at me." She used her hands to present her body like a sexy model at the car show would.

As Bryce stared at her, she could hear the homebuilder shouting over the phone, "Bryce, are you there? Can you hear me?"

Finally, Bryce mumbled yes as he almost started drooling.

He asked Bryce, "Can you come repair a house? It is closing today, and you would make it worth your while. It's a real emergency. The owners will not sign the final papers until this is fixed."

Bryce let out a big sigh. He could not say no. Bryce whispered and mumbled, "I could be there in about an hour."

The builder told Bryce, "Thanks, your saving my neck on this one," and hung up the phone.

Bryce heard Jamie turn the shower on. Bryce thought, *This moment has never been happier.* He didn't want to leave or the night and morning to end.

Jamie had been listening. She stuck her head out of the bathroom door with her toothbrush in her mouth and said, "Are you sure you have to go?"

Bryce just nodded his head up and down and said, "He helped me when I needed help, so I can help him if he needs help."

Jamie just said, "Okay," then she pushed the door open and said, "I'm going to take a shower." She stood in full view of Bryce. She turned, spit into the sink, rinsing her mouth, looking over her right should and winked at Bryce. She opened the shower door and started to get in.

Bryce jumped out of bed and ran into the shower with her. He kissed her, then they made love in the shower. Bryce held to the handrail while they were making love, then they washed each other's body.

He said to Jamie, "I guess I'm skipping breakfast this morning?"

She just smiled.

"Last night, I will never forget. Do you want to do it again tonight?" he said.

"I'll take you up on that," she said playfully. "Now get out of here. I have to go to work."

Bryce got out of the shower, put his clothes on, ran out of the house, got into his truck, and sped to the job site.

*****

As Bryce was pulling into the driveway at the job site, a gun was taken out of the ear of the builder. Four members of the dogs had held him down and shot him in the head. The leader of the pack is Boxer. He then tells the other dogs to "make it look like the Grip dude did it." So one of the dogs took the dead builder's finger and wrote the name Bryce on the desk in blood.

*****

Bryce had walked up to the trailer door, knocked on it and said, "Hey, it's me. Have you got any of those bricks?" He opened the door, stepped in, and saw the builder lying on the floor. Then he was hit in the back of the head with a tire iron. He was out cold.

Boxer then punched Bryce in the nose. Blood trickled out of his nose. He grabbed the dead builder's hand and rubbed his knuckles across his face, smearing the blood. Boxer was really proud of himself.

He said, "That will fix him! Now get him in the car and let's get out of here."

*****

Jose had arrived for work. Walking up behind the trailer, he saw four men dragging Bryce and shoving him into a car. He ducked down behind the trash dumpster so they couldn't see him. As they drove away, he ran to the door looked inside and saw the builder lying on the floor. He did not know what to do. He looked around to see if anybody was looking. He then walked back home. He was afraid he would be accused or sent back home to Mexico.

CHAPTER 6

Officer Veal received a phone call. Officer Veal walked over to the captain's office and knocked on the door and stepped inside. He then said to his captain, "There is a disturbance at a new home construction site. Do you want me to check it out?"

The captain said, "Yes, take a uniform with you."

When Officer Veal and the uniformed officer arrived at the job site and walked into the trailer, the two officers saw a dead man lying on the floor. Officer Veal told the uniformed officer, "Call the crime scene investigators. Don't touch a thing and put an APB on Bryce Hix."

The young police officer said, "How do you know that?"

Officer Veal pointed at the name written in blood on the desk.

"But how do you know it's Bryce Hix?"

"Just do it!" Officer Veal yelled at the officer.

The young police officer radioed in like he was told. Officer Jones heard the report over the radio. He immediately called Jamie. He was relieved when she answered. He asked, "When was the last time you saw Bryce?"

Reluctantly, she said, "About an hour ago. He left to go to work. He had to meet the builder at the construction site."

Officer Jones said, "The one on Peoria Street?"

She said, "Yes."

"You better get down there. I'll meet you."

Before she could ask what had happened, he hung up the phone. Jamie frantically finished getting dressed, jumped in her car, and sped off with her siren blaring.

When she arrived, Officer Jones was already there talking to Officer Veal. Jamie burst into the trailer. She shouted, "What happened? Where is Bryce?"

Officer Veal blurted out, "Your boyfriend murdered this man and is on the run." He then turned to Officer Jones. "He won't get away with this crime. I will see it through!"

Jamie grabbed Officer Veal, slamming him into the wall. "Everyone here knows you're a crooked cop!"

Officer Jones pulled Jamie off Officer Veal and said, "Easy, Dirty Harriet. He isn't worth it." He then said, "What the hell?" and punched Officer Veal in the nose.

Officer Veal fell out the door of the trailer. He got up and said, "You will pay for that, Jones."

Officer Jones shouted back, "Whatever the cost, that was worth it."

The captain walked up and said, "What the hell is going on here?"

Officer Veal said, "Those two morons don't like what the truth is, so they're taking it out on me."

Jamie shouted at the captain, "He claims Bryce did this. Why would he kill him? He worked for him. Captain, his truck is still here. How did he leave? And look at all the footprints and the drag marks, like someone was being dragged, and these tire tracks were someone peeled out." Jamie pointed to the ground.

The captain looked at Officer Veal and said, "How do you explain putting an APB on someone without all the facts?"

Officer Veal replied, "The victims spelled out his name on the desk, and his blood is on his hand."

Officer Jones answered, "How many victims that have been shot in the back of the head with their brains scattered everywhere can miraculously spell out the killer's name? He couldn't have the motor function to do that, and how the hell do you know that's Bryce's blood? Are you psychic?"

Veal said, "It has to be his."

Jamie said, "This is just too perfect. What a setup. Somebody's trying to frame him. Can't you see that?"

The captain said, "Okay, this thing stinks. Jones, you take over the investigation. And, Bell, you stay away from this investigation. You're emotionally involved."

Jamie threw up her hands and stomped off.

Officer Veal screamed at the captain, "This is my case, you can't—"

Before he could finish the sentence, the captain stuck his finger in the face of Officer Veal and said, "Shut your mouth. I am your superior officer. I can shit down your neck if I want to. I don't know if you're a dirty cop or not. There's never been any proof of that to me. That doesn't mean you're not a stupid cop."

Officer Veal stomped to his car, slammed his door, and sped off. Three blocks away, he pulled into a convenient store, pulled out his cell phone, and called Poodle.

Poodle answered, "What's up, BC?"

Officer Veal shouted, "The next time you call me with information, let someone with intelligence talk to me. Your idiot dogs made me look like a fool. The captain ain't buying a murder rap on Hix, so you better get rid of him, and you owe me big!" Officer Veal hung up the phone.

*****

Five minutes later José showed up. He was feeling guilty about what he saw. He came up to Jamie and said, "I see something."

Jamie said, "What did you see?"

Jose did not speak English very well, "I see Bryce. Four men put him in car and drive away."

She asked, "Was he okay?"

"No, they carry him," José replied.

She said, "Do you know who it was?"

He pointed to the ground and drew a paw print, the symbol of the gang.

Jamie said, "The dogs?"

He nodded his head. She took him over to Officer Jones. She told Officer Jones what he said to her. Officer Jones who knew Spanish spoke to him in Spanish for a minute or two. He was satisfied with what he had said.

Jamie was worried. She kept asking Officer Jones, "What did he say? What did you say?"

Officer Jones replied, "Calm down. He said basically the same thing you did."

"So let's go. Let's bust some dogs' heads," she said.

"Wait a minute, Jamie, you can't go. You heard the captain."

Jamie looked at Officer Jones and glared, "You can't keep me from this, you can't."

Officer Jones, against his better judgment, said, "Okay, but you stick with me. You don't say a word, and if you get in any trouble, you're out."

She nodded her head and said, "Let's go."

They drove to a local hangout or bar where the dogs frequent. It was called The Kennel, a very rough part of town. The police rarely go there because any disturbance at The Kennel was always handled in the bar. They never called the police. Two back-up police cars pulled up beside of them.

Officer Jones pointed. "You go to the back door, and you follow us."

Officer Jones and Jamie walked right through the front door, and immediately two young men took off running. Jamie tackled one and held him on the ground. Officer Jones clothes lined the other, hitting him right across the face, knocking him to the ground.

Jamie put her handcuffs on the young man, asking him, "Where are you going, dog? Do you know something?" Squeezing the cuffs extra tight until the young man shouted at her, "Those are too tight, bitch."

Jamie grabbed the back of the young man's hair and pulled his head up. She gritted her teeth and whispered, "I'm not your bitch," then shoved his face back into the floor.

Officer Jones helped the other young man to his feet. "Going somewhere?" he asked. "What's your name?"

The young man rubbed his nose and said, "My name is Beagle."

And the one on the ground that Jamie was sitting on blurted out, "His name? My name is Mutt."

"Why did you take off running the split second we walked into the bar?"

"I just figured you would say we did something wrong," Beagle said.

"Well, maybe you did. There was a murder at the construction site. We might be able to pin that on you if you don't answer some questions. There was a man named Bryce Hix. We have got good information that the dogs have him. Now you give us his location, you walk out of here," Officer Jones said.

Mutt said, "The big dog wants him. Everybody knows that."

The Beagle kicked Mutt in the head and shouted, "What are you doing, dog? Don't tell them shit!"

Jamie stood up on the back of the young man and kicked Beagle in the head. She said, "Does not feel so good, does it?" She then pulled her gun and stuck it up his nose, then pulled it back and cracked him over the head. He fell to the ground, and he was out cold.

Officer Jones turned to Jamie and said, "I've never seen this side of you, partner. I like it." He smiled. "I hope if I was kidnapped, you would be this pissed off too."

Jamie stuck her foot into the back of the neck of the dog on the floor. "Talk," she said, "or I'll put a bullet in the back of your head and say you were resisting arrest."

The man shouted from the floor, "That dude is going to die. He messed with the big dog."

Officer Jones kneeled down and asked, "Where is he? Or I will turn Dirty Harriet loose on you."

The Mutt answered, "No one knows, and man, if I told you, I would be dead."

A crowd was gathering in the bar toward the back. Random patrons in the crowd were shouting at the young men in custody, saying things like, "You dogs better quit whimpering because the big dog is going to bite your ass."

Four other police officers came in the back door and started milling through the crowd, poking them with their batons and telling them to "Shut up!"

"Then who do we need to talk to, to find out?" Officer Jones said.

"The only dog who might know is Poodle or his snitch cop. Don't know his name, but they call him BC. I don't know why? That's all I know. Can you take her foot out of my neck now?"

Beagle shouted, "Shut up, dog," and tried to stomp on his head.

But Jamie quickly side kicked him in the balls. He fell to the ground, coughing and holding himself.

"The policeman you called BC, have you ever seen his face or what does that stand for?" Officer Jones asked.

"The only dog who knows him is Poodle, and I don't know what it stands for."

One of the men from the crowd shouted, "You're a dead dog," pointing his fist at Mutt. But he was silenced by one of the police officers with a baton to the stomach.

Officer Jones stood up and said, "Let him go, partner."

She pulled her foot off his neck and helped him up. She pushed him toward one of the uniformed officers and said, "Take him in." She walked over to the other young man who was sitting up. She stuck her gun in his mouth. She said angrily, "You're going to tell me something, or you're going to eat one of my bullets."

His eyes got big as cue balls. He mumbled something.

Jamie pulled the gun out of his mouth and said, "Say it again. Try talking without the gun in your mouth, maybe we can understand you." She then put the gun in the crotch of his pants. "I can shoot you here. They would believe you were running away, and I shot you in the balls."

The young man said at a whisper, "I know what BC stands for. It means Baby Cow."

Officer Jones looked puzzled and said, "What the hell does baby cow mean?"

Jamie pulled her gun and said, "I know who it is. Let's go talk to him."

Officer Jones pulled Beagle up by his hair and whispered in his ear, "We are taking you and Mutt in for your protection, but my advice is get out of town!"

As they left, Officer Jones kept asking, "Who is it? Tell me."

She turned to him as they sat down in her car. "Baby cow. It's Officer Veal. It has to be," she said.

Officer Jones replied, "That fucking Veal. No wonder the dogs called him. That's why he knew. Two types of blood. No one could look at a crime scene and determine that!"

*****

On the other side of town, in an abandoned warehouse next to the pier, Bryce woke up. His hands were tied around an old wooden cable spool. He could hardly see from the beating he had taken. Four dogs were playing dominoes at a card table.

The big dog walked in and said, "How's the boy doing?" He walked over to him, lifted his head, and said, "You see this hand," showing him the hand with a cast on it. "You're going to wish you'd never touched this hand" He then slapped Bryce across the face with the cast. "You are going to suffer before you die. You're going to wish for my bullet to the head."

Bryce then dropped his head. He noticed he couldn't move his feet. They were in a tub of concrete. He tried to wiggle his feet. They've moved a little, so he kept trying to wiggle them to loosen the concrete. It was not completely dry yet so, we kept working them.

Doberman walked over to the table and whispered something into one of the dogs' ear. He nodded his head, then Doberman left the warehouse, jumped in his new Hummer and drove off.

One of the dogs then hollered out to Bryce. He said, "Yo, Bryce, wake up. It's time for your hourly beating."

The other gang members all laughed.

One of them walked over to him, raised his head up, and said,

"This dude is half dead." He dropped his head. "Let's get back to the game." They started playing again.

Then a few minutes later, Doberman's Hummer returned. He jumped out of the vehicle and walked hurriedly to the table and said, "There is a change of plans. We're going to have to cut this short. The police are closing in. Let's go ahead and get rid of him like I planned."

He walked over to Bryce, lifted his head up, and said, "It won't be long now. It's almost over for you, but just remember your mama is next."

Bryce thought about trying to get free but just played possum instead.

Doberman then smacked him across the face again, unzipped his pants, and pissed all over Bryce. "I do this every time to mark my scent before you die." He then zipped up, started walking away, and shouted, "Take care of this now!" He then got back in his Hummer and drove off.

One of the dogs said, "I hate when he does that. Man, there is nothing worse than a man that's been pissed on. Let's get the dolly and just roll him on to the boat."

A few moments later the two dogs came back with the dolly. They untied Bryce from the wooden spool and strapped him to the dolly. One of the dogs pulled the strap until Bryce grunted.

"There that's tight enough," the young man said.

The four dogs wheeled Bryce to the boat, put him inside, and laid him down on the deck. Bryce couldn't move. He tried to open his eyes, but he was blinded by the afternoon sun. They started the motor and drove out to sea. After driving a while, one asked, "How far out should we go?"

Another said, "Far enough he'll never be found. Besides he's going to be fish food anyway."

As they drove farther and farther, Bryce knew he was on a boat but didn't know where. The motor stopped. He heard the anchor splash into the water.

He thought, *This is it. I've got to get out of here somehow.*

They wheeled him to the other side of the deck. They pulled the gate before they threw him over. One of the dogs hit Bryce four times in the face. Bryce was woozy again and nearly unconscious. They started to throw him in, but one of the dogs yelled, "Stop! Take him off that dolly. That's my dolly!"

They untied him. Two of the dogs lifted him up. He was very heavy because of the concrete on his feet. Another one cut Bryce on the arm, so he was bleeding heavily.

He said, "This should bring the sharks," and he laughed.

They shoved him over the side. The cool water hitting Bryce's face helped bring Bryce around. His mind was spinning on the way down, searching for any way out! His arms and hands were reaching frantically for a miracle.

On the deck of the boat, the other dogs were dumping out fish chum to attract more sharks. They started the motor a few times to stir up the chum. Bryce was nearly out of breath and gasping for air when he saw the anchor dragging by him. He quickly grabbed it. It was dragging him along with the boat, then it started pulling him up. He hung on. The twin motors were picking up speed. Now the anchor was heading by the motors. Bryce then swung his feet toward the motor propellers. It was his last-ditch effort. He was hoping for some kind of miracle. The wash tub full of concrete hit the propellers, busting the tub and the concrete apart. He pulled his feet out while the propellers were jammed against the wash tub. As the motor stopped, the dogs onboard were wondering what the hell had happened or what hit the boat. They tilted up the boat motors. They could see that the propellers were all twisted and bent.

One of the dogs said, "We must've hit a fish or a sea turtle or something."

They tried the motor again. The propellers started turning.

"Just take it easy," one of them said. "We don't want to be stuck out here. Let's get as far away from here as we can go and radio the big dog."

The young dog went downstairs picked up the radio. He then noticed there was blood on the floor. Bryce came from behind the door and grabbed him around the throat with both hands and snapped his neck like a twig without a struggle. Bryce took the jacket off the limp body of the young man. He started wiping the blood off his feet and arm. A roll of duct tape was lying on the counter. As Bryce reached for the tape, a knife fell out of the jacket. It was a switch blade. He quickly wrapped tape around his feet and the bloody cut on his arm. Bryce started to get up but looked at the dog's shoes. Bryce grabbed the foot of the dog and sized the bottom of the shoe to his foot. Bryce's foot was about two sizes too small, but it would have to do. He untied the shoes and quickly put them onto his feet, pulling the shoe strings as tight as he could. Bryce got to his knees but picked up the switch blade knife before standing. Bryce pushed the button on the knife. It opened in an instance. Holding the knife, Bryce reached for the counter with the other hand, pulling himself up. Standing for a few seconds, he felt a little woozy. He started up the stairs quietly. Suddenly, one of the dogs opened the cabin door and met Bryce face-to-face. Bryce stabbed him in the chest with the knife.

The dog shouted at the gang member on the boat deck, "Shoot him, shoot him!" The gang member on the deck pulled a 9mm out of his pants while running to the doorway. He could see Bryce. He pointed and started firing. Bryce quickly grabbed the guy he just stabbed and used him as a shield. He screamed with pain as he was shot in the back five times. Bryce, with all of his strength, shoved the dead body out the door and onto the dog who was shooting at him. They fell to the ground. Bryce jumped on top. He grabbed the hand that held the gun and squeezed the hand around the gun. He heard bones cracking as the dog shouted in pain. Then he easily pulled the gun from his hand and threw it overboard. Bryce then grabbed his throat and was choking him. The eyes were rolling back in the head of the gang member. Suddenly, Bryce was hit in the back of the head with an oar. He rolled away to avoid the next swing. It missed. He quickly got to his feet. The dog kept Bryce at a distance with the ore swinging at him. He then yelled at the other dog, "Get up! Get up! Get your gun and shoot the bastard." The dog, with a broken hand, lying on the deck of the boat was struggling to get up while the other kept swinging at Bryce to keep him away. Bryce picked up a life preserver and was protecting himself with it. Finally, a real hard swing came at Bryce. He caught it in the hole of the life preserver, then grabbed it. The dog was no match for Bryce's grip. He ripped it from him and broke it in half across his knee, then threw it at the dog. It stabbed him in the stomach. The dog fell to the ground. Blood oozed out of his fingers as he tried to remove the oar. Moaning over and over, "Help me, help me." The other dog struggled to his feet, and Bryce hit him over the head with the other half of the broken oar. The dog fell to the deck. Bryce then picked him up and threw him overboard, then walked over to the other man who was bleeding all over the deck. He was pleading with Bryce.

He whimpered, "Help me, man, don't kill me!"

Bryce grabbed him by the arm, pulled him to the side of the boat, held him over, and said, "Fish food, remember?" and dropped him. Bryce pulled each dog to the side of the boat and pushed them over. Bryce went down to use the radio, picking up the microphone, panting, saying, "Mayday, mayday. Is anyone out there?"

All he could hear was static. As he looked over the radio, he could see it was hit by gunfire. Bryce slammed the microphone down and shouted, "I can't get a fucking break." Bryce went back on the deck to the steering wheel. Bryce started the engine. It sounded awful. The higher he pulled back on the throttle, the worse it sounded. Bryce looked up at the sun. He figured it was about three o'clock on the afternoon. Then he shouted at himself, "You dumb shit, why didn't you check those bastards for cell phones before throwing them over the side."

Bryce was so fatigued. He pointed the boat west and tied the steering wheel with the strap of a life preserve. The boat was traveling about five miles an hour. Bryce sat down on the deck of the boat, leaning next to the chair. "I'll just rest a minute or two." He was out exhausted.

CHAPTER 7

At the police station, Jamie and Officer Jones were looking for a police officer. They both said at the same time, "Where's Veal?"

The captain said, "I sent him on a two-week vacation before we transfer him out of here."

Officer Jones slammed his fist down on the desk. "We need him!" he shouted.

Jamie said, "Pull his file, find his address."

"What's going on?" the captain said.

"We think he's the informer to the dogs."

"What proof do you have?" the captain said.

"We have one of the gang members. He gave us his code name. They call him BC, which stands for baby cow."

The captain nodded his head. He turned to the computer on his desk. He typed in Officer Veal's name. Officer Veal's badge number came up with all other information about him. The captain pointed to the screen, "There it is, the address." The captain wrote it down on his pad and started to hand it to Officer Jones but pulled it back and glared at Officer Jones and Jamie. He said to them, "I want him brought to me not beat up. Don't let him know why we want him. Make up some story, but get him here without any incident. You got it? Take another unit with you. Tell them nothing. Let them knock on his door. Don't act crazy. Just get him here!" As Jamie and Officer

Jones left his office, the captain shouted at Jamie, "Officer Bell, you calm down!"

Walking down the hall, Officer Jones said to Jamie, "Let's tell the officers that Veal has to come in and sign some paperwork about his transfer before his vacation. Captain's orders."

Jamie nodded her head and said, "Sounds good. Let's roll."

Officer Jones approached two officers who had just come on duty. He told them to come outside. Walking over to the squad car, Officer Jones said, "We have to go to Officer Veal's house. His life may be in danger. Me and Officer Bell will be your backup. Just go to his front door, tell Veal the captain needs him to come in pronto about his transfer papers. They must be signed today. We don't want to alarm Veal. We want him to get safely to the office before we tell him he's in great danger."

They pulled into Officer Veal's driveway. His car wasn't there. They rang the doorbell, and nobody answered. Officer Jones and Jamie came up to the officers.

The young officer said, "Doesn't look like he's home."

Jamie said, "You go around back and wait until we let you in."

The two officers went to the back of the house.

Officer Jones asked Jamie, "Well, maybe we should just wait here unless you want to kick in the door?"

Without hesitation, Jamie kicked in the door.

Officer Jones looked at Jamie and said, "I was just kidding. This isn't legal. We don't have a warrant."

She said, "No time, we have no time."

As they looked around the house, they noticed a lot of expensive things.

Jamie said to him, "If this guy isn't on the take, I don't know who is. All his clothes are gone. His car is gone. What now?"

He said, "Let's go find Poodle or the big dog. Let's hit the streets."

Jamie opened the back door and told the two officers, "Go back to your beat and keep this quiet. We don't want Veal in any more danger. We will follow up and make sure he just went on vacation."

JIM IVY

As they were leaving, Jamie's cell phone rang. It was Bryce's mother.

"Hello," answered Jamie.

His mother asked, "Have you seen Bryce today? I can't reach him. I'm worried something is wrong."

Jamie said, "Yes, I did. Something's wrong with his phone. He's working late. It's a rush house. He asked me to call you, and I forgot. He might have to work really late. I'm sorry, it's my fault."

Lying to his mother was the only thing she could think of doing because she just didn't know what happened to Bryce.

Jaime then said, "I have to go. I'll see you tomorrow, and I'll have Bryce call you when I see him."

Mrs. Hix said, "Tell him I love him. Good-bye, dear."

Jamie hung up the phone. Her eyes started to tear up.

Officer Jones said to her, "Why did you lie to her? Better yet, you're lying to yourself if you think he is still alive. Jamie, he is dead."

She sat down in the car and started sobbing. She yelled back at Officer Jones, "He is not dead. As long as I feel his heartbeat in my mind. I know every beat and sound it makes from sleeping on his chest. I can feel him. He's alive. I know it, I just know it. I can't hurt his mother. Not yet. Let her believe he's okay just as I do." She then wept on his shoulder.

He caressed her head and said, "You can believe if you want. It's okay, it's okay." And then he said, "You've just gone from Dirty Harriet to a blubbering schoolgirl. It must be love." He shook his head while stroking hers.

*****

Meanwhile, back at the boat, Bryce was now a drift. The motor has quit, and Bryce is at the mercy of the current. Bryce was sitting on the deck of the boat. Every once and in a while he would try and stand and look out over the water, hoping to see a boat or plane. Bryce folded his hands together and prayed, asked for help, and hoped and prayed it would be answered; but the splashing of the waves against the boat was all he heard. He flopped back down on the deck of the boat. Standing made him a little woozy. It would be dark soon.

Bryce thought, *I'll have to go back down the stairs and see if there is any water or food.* But for now he just wanted to rest as he leaned against the captain's chair and fell asleep.

*****

Officer Jones and Jamie had been driving around, checking local hangouts, looking for Poodle or the big dog with no luck. Officer Jones then stopped at the diner they often eat at.

Jamie said, "What are we doing here?"

"Look, you still have to eat or I do. Besides, I have to take a piss," he said.

As Officer Jones went into the bathroom, he pulled out his cell phone and called Randy to tell him what had happened. He said, "Jamie is going to take this hard so be prepared. We're going to need your father and Kelly to help Jamie get through this." He hung up the phone, went to the bathroom, and then went out to get some lunch.

*****

As Randy hung up the phone, he called his father to come over. He told him the situation. His head sank as Randy told him what had happened.

"And your little girl is in pain."

Rock asked Randy, "Where is she?"

He told him, "They were at the diner, but they wouldn't be there long. They had a few more leads to follow, and he would call when they had some news."

Randy said, "At least one thing looks pretty certain. He is dead, and that's the only positive thing about this."

His father said, "How could you get any pleasure from the pain your sister obviously is in? She loves him. Maybe he's alive. Maybe your sister is right."

Randy paused for a few seconds and said, "Dad, Officer Jones was

99 percent sure he was already dead. Four gang members put him in a car. And when it comes to pain, no one enjoys seeing me in pain more than you."

His father stared at him and said, "You know, son, I have tried to give you everything and that's the gratitude I get. You have never appreciated anything I have done for you."

"What do you mean by that, Dad?" Randy responded.

His father answered, "Nothing, just nothing. What about his mother? Have they told her?"

"No, I don't think so," Randy said.

"Maybe I should visit her," Rock said.

"Do what you want, but don't raise any flags," Randy said.

Rock left the gym. Maybe he could comfort Mrs. Hix. He drove to the cancer center and went to her room and knocked on the door.

She answered, "It's about time, get in here."

He pushed the door open. She looked disappointed when he walked into the room. Amy was sitting in her chair with a blue scarf on her head. She had begun to lose her hair.

Rock asked, "Sorry, I guess you were expecting someone else?"

"That's all right," she said. "I was expecting my son. I haven't heard from him today."

Rock said, "Kids, who knows what they are thinking half the time. He's probably with my daughter."

She looked puzzled and said, "No, I called her. She said he was working and his phone wasn't working."

"Well, there you go. He's working," Rock said while smiling like that would satisfy her. Trying to change the subject, Rock asked, "How's your treatment going?"

"Well, I'm losing my hair as you can see, and I'm very tired. I sleep too much, and when I'm out, I'm out for hours," Amy said.

"Well, maybe Bryce came by and you were asleep," Rock said.

"Bryce would have left flowers or balloons or something if he would have come by and I was asleep."

Rock nodded his head and said, "Sounds like a good boy, very thoughtful."

Amy then said, "He really likes Jamie. She'll be good for him. I've never seen him this happy. I think he loves her, and don't worry he will never hurt her."

"That's good to know," Rock said.

As they talked for a while, Rock talked about his life and how hard it was to raise two children after his wife passed away.

"Jamie was ten years old. I let myself become consumed in Randy's wrestling. I know I pushed him too hard. Jamie seemed to enjoy being involved. She would video every match, and then we would watch them together as I critiqued Randy. Jamie even wrestled for a while. Trying to get my attention, I suppose. But then later she took up karate. But in the Olympic trials is when I lost Jamie. At the time, I didn't know why or what had happened between Bryce and Jamie. I was so upset. Bryce was the only man to ever beat my son. I overreacted, I was childish."

Amy replied, talking about raising Bryce, basically by herself after Bryce's father had died. Amy started panting and coughing a little. Her eyes were getting heavy, when Rock butted in and said, "I should go so you can get some rest."

Rock then left the room and went downstairs to the gift shop. He went over to the attendant on duty and said to her, "I know this is going to sound pretty weird, but please don't ask a lot of questions. I'll pay you extra for it." Rock told her the room number and asked the attendant, "Would you send Mrs. Hix some flowers and sign them, 'From your son, Bryce. I didn't want to wake you. Love, Bryce.' Do that today, send balloons tomorrow, and candy the next day. And make sure she's asleep when you bring them." Rock gave the attendant $200.

The attendant nodded and said, "I'll take care of it."

Rock then left the center and drove back to the gym.

*****

Randy said, "You know, I just don't get it here. This guy Bryce comes back into my life, and he is screwing it all up again. You know he is the only man to beat me in anything, and I always thought it was just poetic justice that he got caught cheating and I got to go to the Olympics."

Kelly then said, "How many beers have you had?"

Randy said, "Six."

"Babe, you need some coffee or a sandwich. Let me fix you one," said Kelly.

Randy then said, "It's like everyone is blaming me for all that went wrong with this man's life."

"You're drunk," she said. "And you're awfully cute when you're drunk."

"No, I'm not," he said. "It's just I'll never get the chance to beat him. It has tortured me my whole life."

Kelly gently grabbed him in the face and kissed him and said, "That's a lie. I beat you all the time, at least two or three times a week," while smiling.

He answered, "No, I'd let you win just so I can have your body." He chuckled at himself.

She then hugged him and said, "I'll get the coffee, and I will let you win tonight."

*****

Officer Jones cell phone rang. It was one of his snitches. Officer Jones called him Cowboy because he always wore a Dallas Cowboy hat. Cowboy was homeless, but he always came up with good information for cash. Cowboy called Officer Jones from the free phone at the homeless shelter. He tells him a place where they might find the gang member called Poodle. "He is at a house of one of his girlfriends." He gave him the address, but before he hung up the phone, he said, "Don't forget to bring me my money."

Officer Jones and Jamie drove over to the house. They snuck up to the window and peeked inside. They saw nothing. Then a woman appeared and walked right by the window. She was totally nude and quite stunning.

Jamie poked Officer Jones in the ribs. "Get a good look," she whispered to him.

Officer Jones whispered back, "Let's just say, I could pick her out of any lineup. Let's go in."

They quietly snuck up to the backdoor. It was locked. He took out his credit card and slid it in. The door opened. They crawled in, each having their weapons in hand. They crawled up to the door where they saw the woman go in. Officer Jones looked through the keyhole. The woman was giving oral sex to someone.

He looked at Jamie and said, "Let's go."

They burst in and yelled, "Freeze!"

Poodle reached for his pistol. Officer Jones dove on him and knocked the naked woman out of the way. A struggle over the pistol occurred while the woman screamed.

Jamie slapped her across the face and said, "Shut up." She walked up to Poodle and stuck her gun up his ass and said, "Stop or I will give you a real blow job."

Poodle stopped struggling and just lay there not moving a muscle.

Officer Jones said, "Why did you do that? I had him."

Jamie replied, "Sure you did."

Poodle shouted at them, "I haven't done anything! Who the fuck are you?"

Jamie then cocked her pistol and said, "Now I'll talk. You listen. Just yes or no. Okay?"

He answered, "Yes."

She said, "Is your dog name Poodle?"

"No!" he shouted.

Jamie pulled the trigger. It clicked. She then said, "I forgot how many bullets I put in today. Was it five or four? I can't remember. I'll ask again. Is your name Poodle?"

He said, "Yes."

"Do you know who Bryce Hix is?"

"No!" he shouted.

She starts to pull the trigger again.

He then shouted, "Yes, yes."

"Good boy," she said.

"Do you know where he is?"

He replied, "No, no. I mean, don't shoot. I'm telling the truth."

Officer Jones said to her, "Just plug this punk. It's one less street dog that doesn't know anything."

She cocked her gun again, and Poodle said, "I can find out if he's still alive, just hang on. Give me my cell phone. I can call BC. He might know."

"What does that stand for?" she asked.

He muttered, "Bad Cat."

Again she stuck the barrel of her gun farther up his ass.

He then shouted out, "Baby Cow."

"That's better," she said. "Call him."

He had it on speed dial. Jamie told him to put it on speaker phone. He did.

The phone rang.

BC answered, "Yo, dog, what do you want?"

"Hey, BC, what happened? There are cops all over looking for the dude."

BC answered, "Well, it's done. He took a concrete swim. A lot of heat on this one. It would be better not to talk for a while, dog. I am getting out of town. See you on the flip side." Officer Veal started to hang up but said, "The big dog has one more task to do first. Don't call me again, you dig."

Officer Jones then said, "What task, Veal? Yeah, I dig, Officer Veal."

BC answered, "Hey, don't use my name on a cell phone, stupid shit. The big dog is going to take care of his mother too."

"This isn't Poodle. It's Officer Jones, and you're a dead man."

The phone went dead.

*****

Officer Veal was boarding a plane. He thought, *Well, Jones, you will have to find me.* He walked on the plane with nothing but his carry-on bag that has about $350,000 in it. *I can live quite nice on this*, he thought as he buckled his seatbelt and grinned to himself.

*****

Officer Jones turned to Poodle and whispered, "You better hope Bryce is alive 'cause no one will be able to save you if he's dead."

Jamie shoved the gun hard up Poodles ass and said, "You better be our snitch on Bryce's mother because I will make it my personal goal to see you and big dog dead. So don't run a red light or steal a box of Tic Tacs because I will be there with this gun to finish my blow job, and you better hope the big dog still has Bryce. Now tell me, Poodle, where can we find the big dog?"

Poodle answered, stuttering, "Probably at Lexi's. That's his bitch. She lives uptown, but you'll never get there. He'll be dead before you reach the door. Believe it. If they smell cop. They'll shoot first, and they won't care who gets in the way. A lot of kids and old people are there. It will be a bloodbath."

"Then how do we get in?" Jamie said.

"You don't. No one does, not even me. Doberman has dogs on every corner and all over the building. It's better to get him when he comes out," Poodle said.

"Would Bryce be there?" Jamie said.

"Are you deaf? BC already said he took a concrete swim. It's just a safe house. Nothing illegal is going on there."

"So if we come in with a bunch of cops, what will happen?" Officer Jones said.

"You won't catch him there. He has a secret way out, and no one knows but him. I mean no one."

Jamie pulled the gun out of his ass. She then wiped her gun off on his jacket. She opened the chamber of her gun and clicked out five bullets and said, "You're lucky, dog."

Poodle answered, "No, dead. You better arrest me and put me in jail and her too." He pointed at his girl.

Jamie turned to the girl and asked her, "Where is your family girl?"

She answered, "They don't live here. I left home four years ago."

"Well," Jamie said, "you're going home like it or not." She pointed at Poodle. "You're better off with us."

She put her handcuffs on him and told Poodle, "We will take you downtown and figure out what to do with you later."

"You better put me in solitary confinement because the big dog will pay plenty for my collar."

*****

It had been thirty-six hours since anyone had seen Bryce. No one knew he was alive but adrift in a boat. Officer Jones dropped Jamie off at the cancer center while he took Poodle to the police precinct to place him in protective custody. Jamie went to see Bryce's mother. She knocked on the door.

She answered said, "Come in."

Jamie entered the room and started to say something but noticed the flowers on her table. She stopped to read the card.

"When did you get these?" Jamie asked.

Mrs. Hix said, "Today. Bryce must have brought them while I was asleep."

Jamie looked puzzled, thinking, *Maybe he's alive. Maybe he's hiding. He's hiding from them.* Jamie's heart started beating out of her chest, and she had almost come to the realization that Bryce was dead, but this gave her hope.

Mrs. Hix said, "Have you seen him, dear? I know Bryce must be really busy."

Jamie said, "I've been working a tough case, and I haven't been able to catch him. I just wanted to check on you. I'll see you later." She waved good-bye and stepped out of her room. Jamie went into the hallway and pushed the button for the elevator. She was so keyed up. Jamie took the stairs, running down them as fast as she could. When she reached the bottom floor, she shoved the door open and fast walked down the hall to the gift shop. While panting, she opened the door. She walked up to the attendant on duty.

"Have you been here all day?" Jamie asked.

The attendant answered, "No, I just came on duty. Mary worked this morning. She'll be back in the morning."

Jamie handed her a card with her number on it. "Have Mary call me."

The attendant asked, "Why?"

Jamie just held up her badge and said, "Is that good enough for you?"

The attendant just nodded, and Jamie walked down the hall to the security office. Gus was on duty.

Jamie held up her badge and said, "Show me the security video of the visitors in Amy Hix's room." As Jamie sat there fast-forwarding through, she saw it wasn't Bryce but her father who visited, no one else. She thought, *Maybe Bryce paid the attendant to deliver the flowers.* Then Jamie shouted, "Bryce, where are you?"

CHAPTER 8

Bryce was still adrift, but suddenly he awoke like someone was calling his name. He raised his head over the side of the boat. He could see another boat on the horizon. He fumbled for the flare gun he found below and fired. Hopefully, they would come. It was the only flare, and again Bryce was weak. He had lost a lot of blood. He bandaged his feet as good as he could, but he knew if he did not get help soon he would die. The sound of another boat was coming closer. He could hear it. The waves pounded against his boat.
A voice shouted out, "Ahoy, are you okay?"

They boarded his boat. It was a family of four who were on a vacation, sailing. The father came over quickly to Bryce and gave Bryce a quick once over and said, "Are you okay, sir?"

Bryce just moaned and said, "Help me, please."

The father looked around the boat as his wife came over to Bryce and tried to help. The father quickly came back to his wife and said, "This boat is a mess. It's been shot up, and there is bloodstains everywhere. Just leave him alone. I'll radio the Coast Guard to see if they could come pick him up."

The mother replied, "This man is hurt. He might die. Let me change the dressings on his feet and arm." She shouted to her son, "Bring me the first aid kit." She pulled the bandages from Bryce's feet and arms, then cleaned them and re-bandaged them.

Bryce lay on the deck of the boat motionless while the woman attended to him. Bryce could feel himself slipping and slipping into a deep sleep.

The Coast Guard arrived about an hour later. The family that found Bryce told the lieutenant what they knew, which wasn't much.

The lieutenant thanked the family and said, "We will take it from here."

They brought a stretcher onboard to load Bryce and moved him to their boat and towed the other boat in.

*****

Bryce woke up in a hospital bed with his left hand handcuffed to the bedpost. A young doctor walked into Bryce's room and saw he was awake.

"How are you, sir?" the physician said. "Do you know who you are? What's your name?"

Bryce didn't know what to say, so he played dumb and just said no and rubbed his head.

The doctor then said, "Do you know what happened, and how you got here?"

Again Bryce just said no and asked, "How long have I been here, and what day is it?"

The doctor said, "You've been here about twenty-four hours, and it's Monday."

Bryce then asked, "Why am I handcuffed?"

The doctor answered, "Well, the police did that because they had some questions about how they found you, and I'm supposed to call them when you're awake."

He asked, "Where am I?"

The doctor said, "You're in a small town outside of the city."

Bryce then nodded and said, "I'm tired." He pretended to doze off.

The young doctor then said, "I have called the police. They will have some questions for you." The doctor left the room.

Bryce was thinking, *I have to get out of here. I'm not answering a bunch of questions about this. It might just lead them to me again. I need for them to think I'm dead, then I will have the advantage.* So Bryce then took his right hand and put it on the two bars that the handcuffs were attached to and squeezed the bar until it broke, then slipped the handcuffs off the bar. He got up, looked into the closet, and realized he had no clothes. So he peeked out the door and didn't see anyone and walked down the hallway. He pushed open another door where a man lay sleeping in a hospital bed. Bryce sneaked in quietly and opened the closet door. There were some shoes, shirts, and pants. *Not really my style, but it will have to do.* He put them on. They were a little big but good enough. Then he sneaked back out around the back staircase and went down three flights of stairs. Bryce peeked out the stairway door. He could see two security officers talking.

One of them said, "He was going to do his rounds."

The other said, "He would man the desk and monitors after he went to the bathroom."

Bryce noticed the handcuffs on his belt, then looked at the one on his wrist. He thought, *I have to get this cuff off.* So Bryce stayed back and watched the officer go into the restroom. Bryce followed. The officer hung his belt up over the top of the covered bathroom stall. Bryce went to the urinal as he went to the restroom. Looking at the belt, he could see handcuff keys clipped onto the belt. So Bryce went over turned the water on at the sink. He reached over and opened the clasp on the belt and removed the handcuff keys. He walked over by the running water, took the key, and opened his cuffs. He put the cuffs in his pocket. Suddenly the stool flushed. Knowing he wouldn't have time to put the keys back, Bryce headed for the door and dropped the keys by the door. Bryce quickly walked to the closest exit. Bryce was out of a hospital and on the street.

Now how am I going to get back to the city with no money? Bryce figured he was about forty miles away. Walking down the street, he saw a truck driver just getting into his big rig. He ran over to him and asked, "Are you going to the city?"

The truck driver said, "Yes."

"Can I bum a ride? I have no money."

The truck driver paused and said, "Sure, why not? Listen, don't try anything funny. I have a gun." He showed it to Bryce.

Bryce said, "Don't worry, I just need to get to the city."

Bryce sat in silence as the truck driver rambled on and on about various things from politics to sports. Bryce didn't want to be rude, so occasionally he nodded his head and said a few things like, "You're right," trying to be agreeable. After all the driver was giving him a ride.

About fifty minutes later, they were in the city.

He asked Bryce, "Where you need to go?"

Bryce told him the address of the construction site. The truck driver punched the address into his GPS. Then the driver told Bryce he could get him within a block or two. The driver pulled over into a parking lot and pointed to Bryce the construction site. It was is about two blocks west. Bryce then got out of the truck, thanked the truck driver, and shook his hand.

The truck driver said, "Wow, that's some grip."

Bryce said, "I know, believe me, I know."

Bryce quickly walked down the street, hoping his truck would still be there. When Bryce arrived, his truck was gone. It must have been impounded by the police. He went around the back of the construction shack and found the hidden key. He went inside, changed his clothes, and found the money he had stashed. Sliding the loose change on the table by his cot in his hand and putting it in his pocket, Bryce quickly put his boots on and then slipped out the back door, down the street to a phone booth outside a convenience store. Bryce fumbled in his pocket for the change, first dialing information to get the number of the cancer center. After getting the number, Bryce hung up the phone, then repeated the number to himself as he dialed.

The operator answered. Bryce asked for the nurse's station on his mother's floor. Bryce talked to the nurse about his mother.

She told him, "She is fine and doing well."

He asked the nurse, "Will you transfer the call to her room."

The phone rang two times, and Jamie answered, "Hello."

Bryce was startled. He didn't know what to do. He just said, "Hey, I'm alive and I'm okay, but I want to keep a low profile for a while."

A couple of tears rolled down Jamie's face, and her nose started to run. A great relief was lifted off her heart. She felt it all along that he was alive.

Mrs. Hix came out of the bathroom. She took one look at Jamie and said, "Give me the phone." She extended her hand while walking gingerly toward Jamie.

She said, "Son."

Bryce answered, "Yes."

Mrs. Hix answered back, "Where are you? I haven't seen you in days. I have lost track of time because of my treatment. It seems I sleep all the time. I was beginning to worry, but I did receive a gift from you every day which let me know you were here."

Bryce was puzzled, not knowing what she was talking about. He then asked her not to worry, that he was really busy and he would see her soon.

He said, "Tell Jamie to meet me at her place in about one hour. It will take me that long to get there. I love you, Mom."

He hung up the phone. Bryce put his sunglasses on and pulled his hooded sweatshirt up over his head and started walking to Jamie's house. Bryce walked at a slow pace. Normally, he would jog but the bandages on his feet made his work boots a little tight, and running made his feet hurt more.

An hour later he arrived at Jamie's. He walked up to the door. It opened. Jamie pulled him in to the house and kissed and hugged Bryce. Jamie's heart was pounding out of her chest. She panted with every breath when she said, "I knew you were alive. What happened?"

So Bryce then told her what had happened, and when he was finished, Jamie said, "I need to call the captain and get an arrest warrant. We can go get Doberman. This will put him away!"

Bryce looked at her and said, "Wait a minute, I'm not here. I'm dead, remember."

Jamie looked puzzled and said, "What do you mean?"

Bryce said angrily, "I'm going to get that bastard. You're right, but not that way. I'm going to kill him with my bare hands."

Jamie's jaw dropped and said, "You can't do this. Are you wanting me to help you kill him?"

"No," he said, "just help me find him. I will do the rest."

Jamie just shook her head and said, "No, I'm not going to do that. I'm a police officer. I swore to uphold the law, not break the law. If you don't stop this, I'm going to arrest you for your own good."

Bryce stared into Jamie's eyes. He said, "You don't know what you're up against. He's going after my mom next. He told me that. I have to find him first."

"But, Bryce, we have security all around her. He knows we are looking for him for your disappearance and the murder of the homebuilder. We will get him, just give us some time."

Bryce shouted, "You've had three days since I was taken, and you haven't found him yet."

There was now a silence in the room. They couldn't even look at each other. Both of them felt they were right. She pulled Bryce to her, grabbing him around the waist. Jamie then ducked her head, trying to get Bryce to look into her eyes. She said, "I can't help you this way. I'm sorry, I can't."

Bryce said, "Well, I'm sorry too." He pulled away, opened the door, crushing the inside doorknob in his anger, and slammed the door behind him as he left.

She yelled out the door, "I'll arrest you the next time I see you!" Jamie tried to follow, but she couldn't open the door. The doorknob was crushed. She kicked at her front door repeatedly, but it did not open. Quickly, she ran to the back door. She opened it and ran around to the front of her house, looking down her street, first to the left and then to the right. There was no sign of Bryce. The only place Bryce could go was back to the cancer center to see his mother.

*****

Bryce walked down a old alleyway, trying to stay out of sight,

JIM IVY

while coming to the end. He can see a city bus parked at a bus stop. Bryce half jogged to the open door, took a step up in the doorway, and asked the driver if his route went by the cancer research center.

The driver answered, "I can get you within a block."

Bryce answered, "Perfect," pulling some change out of his pocket. He then put money in the change dispenser. He sat down behind the driver and said, "Let me know when were there."

The driver nodded.

About forty-five minutes later the bus pulled over to a stop. The driver turned around to Bryce and pointed. He said, "Walk about a block east. You will run right into the hospital."

Bryce said, "Thanks." He stepped off the bus and walk down the street back to the cancer center.

When Bryce walked into the center, the first thing he noticed was more security officers. He then walked over to the elevator and pushed the button. A security officer came up behind Bryce and asked if he could help him.

Bryce answered, "I'm going upstairs to see my mother."

The officer started to question Bryce when Officer Dallas came from the security office. He shouted to the officer, "Let him go," and waved at Bryce.

Bryce gave Officer Dallas a little half wave and a nod of his head before stepping inside the elevator. The ride upstairs to see his mother was long, it seemed. He knocked on the door.

His mother said, "Come in."

Her voice was like sweet music. He walked over to her.

She threw open her arms and hugged him. She said, "I'm glad you are all right. I was worried."

They just held each other for a few seconds.

He said, "There's a good chance I might be arrested again." He then told her why.

She just listened quietly.

"I couldn't make Jamie understand why I need to do this."

His mother paused and said, "Maybe you need to let the police handle this like Jaime said. I will be all right in a couple of weeks.

We can go home. Let the police protect you till they get the people who took you like she said. I mean it, son. Sometimes your pride gets the best of you. Why don't you go to the coffee shop, eat a sandwich, and calm down. I bet if you really listen to her, you will realize she is right."

He then gave his mom a kiss and walked out of her room and down the hall to the restroom after using the restroom. Bryce went to the sink to wash his hands. He stared at himself in the mirror. Bryce then started talking to his reflection.

He said, "Mom and Jamie are right. My place is here with my mother. Maybe I can stay here in my mom's room, and if those bastards step one foot into my mom's room, then I will handle it."

He nodded his head back and forth, pulled some paper towels, dried his hands, and did what his mom said. He went downstairs to the coffee shop. He ordered a burger and fries and sat there alone at a table looking out a window. He could see a fountain. He just stared at it. He pulled out some change and went to the payphone. He called Jamie. He told her maybe she was right. "Just give me some time here with my mom, then you can do what you want."

Jaime said, "I will wait two hours and come get you. Maybe they will put you in my custody till we get Doberman."

Bryce agreed. They hung up the phone. As he was looking out the window, he noticed it had started raining and the wind picked up. He saw lightning far off. He thought, *Great, a thunderstorm. What else could go wrong?*

*****

Upstairs, his mother was sleeping. The rain always calmed her. The rain reminded her of when she was a young girl in the tin roof of her home.

Outside her window a glass cutter was being used. The dogs had stolen a lineman's truck with a basket lift. They had risen up to her window. Quietly they removed the glass and sneaked into her room. One of the dogs had a bottle of chloroform. They splashed onto a towel and then held it over her mouth. She struggled briefly, but she was out quickly. They lifted her to the basket, and then they lowered it to the ground. They put her inside the truck, and they were gone. A note was left.

*****

Bryce came back to the room. His mother was gone.

He shouted, "Mom, are you in the bathroom?" He knocked on the door. He opened the door, and in the mirror was a note written in soap. It said, "We know you're alive. We have your mother. No cops! Ruff-ruff!" A cell phone was also taped to the mirror. Bryce was in a panic. He didn't know what to do. He immediately ran downstairs and out to the parking lot.

A cab driver was sitting in the shade. Bryce ran over to him, opened the door, and got into the back. The driver turned to him and said, "I'm on break. Come back in fifteen minutes."

Bryce grabbed him by the arm and squeezed it and said, "Your break is over."

The cab driver grimaced and said, "Okay, okay, let go." After rubbing his arm, the cab driver said, "Where to?"

"Take me to the police impound yard."

The cab driver nodded his head and said, "I will take you there, but I'm sure they are closed."

Bryce replied, "Just do it."

He arrived at the impound yard, paid the cab driver, tipped him $20, and said, "Sorry about your arm." Bryce then walked to the fence. After looking around, he spotted his truck. He climbed the fence, put his jacket over the barbed wire, and jumped down. He ducked down, keeping his head low, sneaking through the other cars. He could see a security guard station, but the guard was reading the paper. He crawled to his truck, then he crawled under his truck where he had hidden a key. He pulled it out. While crouching, he opened the door. He slipped in quietly and shut the door. He popped his head up. The guard was still reading. He then pulled up his back seat. A secret compartment was there. He opened it. In the compartment was a long hunting knife with a jagged teeth on one side and a gun case. He pulled the case out. Now it was a shotgun with three barrel attachments. He quietly attached the short barrel, which made it look like a sawed-off shotgun. He then loaded the gun and put all of his shells into his hunting vest. He then popped his head up and looked for the best way out. As he looked, he spotted a empty space in front of the fence. He thought, *That's it. I will have to crash through the fence right there.* Bryce looked back in his truck and grabbed his wire cutters. Sneaking between the cars, Bryce arrived at the fence. Bryce cut the wire high enough for his truck to fit through, then he sneaked back to his truck. Bryce put his key into the ignition and started his truck. He drove slowly through the lot and pulled right in front of the open space. He got out of his truck. He looked back. The guard still hasn't moved. He quietly got back in his truck. He looked back toward the guard. He was gone. He could see the guard walking through the lot. He had a clipboard in his hand, and he was counting cars.

Suddenly, the guard noticed a truck was running. He started running toward the truck. The guard pulled out his gun and pointed it at the truck and said, "Freeze, out of the car. Out of the car," he repeated. When he got closer to the truck, he noticed no one in the cab. And then he felt a gun sticking in his pants.

A quiet voice said, "Drop the gun into the cab or I will blow your balls off."

The security guard thought, *This is a $10.50 an hour job. It was not worth my balls."* So he dropped his gun.

Bryce then told the guard to lie on the ground, and he did. Bryce crawled out from under his truck and took the guard's handcuffs and put them onto the security guard. He then got some duct tape and taped his mouth. Bryce broke the window of the car next to his truck with the butt of his shotgun. He then told the guard to lie down in the back seat. Then he taped his feet together and shut the door. Bryce pushed the fence down with his truck. He then lifted the fence back up, taped it with duct tape, and then drove away.

Suddenly, the cell phone rang. It was one of the dogs. They told him where to go to, the old fish cannery at Pier 8, and he had forty-five minutes to get there or his mother would be dead and no police. That's all they said. He quickly called Jamie and asked her to meet him in front of the cancer center in five minutes. Then the phone he had went dead. He peeled out of the lot.

He pulled into the cancer center. Jamie was walking up. He pulled beside her. He opened the door and yelled, "Get in now!"

She said, "How did you get your truck?"

He pulled his shotgun out and repeated, "Get in now!"

She got in to the truck and slammed the door. He handed her the shotgun as he sped off. She started to speak, but he said, "Be quiet and listen. They took my mom to the old fish cannery at Pier 8. Do you have your gun?"

She nodded yes.

"I have thirty-eight minutes to get where I'm supposed to be or they will kill her. No police, they said."

She replied, "It will probably take forty minutes to get there."

Bryce then floored it. Jaime then pulled out her cell phone and started to call. He grabbed it and threw it into the back seat. "No police," he said. "Just you and me, okay? We're going to get her."

Jamie's phone was in the process of calling Officer Jones. He had picked up and started to say "Hello" when Jamie shouted out, "Turn here. It's a quicker way to the old fish cannery at Pier 8." Officer Jones just listened. He knew she was in some kind of trouble. Officer Jones covered the phone with his hand and told Randy, "Get in. Jamie is in some kind of trouble."

Then he heard Jamie say, "What's the plan, Bryce?"

"So far, I am going to crash the gate and drive through. Shoot every dog I see till I find my mom."

She replied, "Not much of a plan!"

He said, "You have a better one."

She said, "Let's call the police."

Bryce shouted, "They will kill her if we storm the place with fifty cops! No, they would be watching as soon as we hit the pier. So before we get there, you duck your head so it looks like I'm alone."

As they got close, Jamie ducked down in the seat as Bryce was driving about eighty miles an hour down the pier to the cannery.

A dog gang member called Doberman and said, "Here he comes, and he's flying, man."

Doberman called down to the gate and told the dogs, "Bring him to me." He hung up the phone.

As Bryce got close to the gate, he slowed down and put his truck into a four-wheel drive. As the dogs were walking toward him, their guns were pointed at him. Bryce put his hands up in the air, and when the four gunmen were ten feet in front of him, he said to Jamie, "We have to go!" He then floored his accelerator to the floor. He hit two of the dogs, and the others jumped out of the way. He crashed through the gate by plowing through barrels and boxes.

Now gunfire opened up. Bullets were flying everywhere in his truck, and Jamie pulled up and fired, killing the first gang member she saw as Bryce pounded through, keeping his foot floored, tearing through everything. Gang members were firing all in the truck, peppering it with bullets, but they could not stop it.

Doberman was watching all this with his video surveillance camera. He told one of his gang members to take his Hummer and stop him. "I mean, crash my Hummer into his truck and stop the bastard and when they get out, sick my babies on them." Doberman was talking about his pit bulls. "I want that son of a bitch alive." He turned to Bryce's mother and said, "That son of yours doesn't quit, does he?"

She paused, then said, "When you're dead, he'll quit."

He glared at her and said, "The bitch. He will be dead and so will you."

The gang member started the Hummer and loaded up four pit bulls with spiked collars. They were taught to attack police or anyone who didn't wear a dog jacket. A big garage door opened, and the Hummer pulled out. The driver waited a few seconds before punching the accelerator. The driver wanted Bryce to get past him a little so he could blindside Bryce. He saw the Toyota Tundra plowing through. He hit the gas.

Bryce yelled out, "Oh shit!"

The Hummer crashed into him and rolled his truck. It landed on the side. Bryce and Jamie crawled out of the passenger side door, jumping behind the truck, using it for cover in the gun battle, firing on anything that moved. The Hummer doors opened, and the pit bulls leaped out and started for Bryce and Jamie. The first pit bull pounced on Jamie's back, pushing her to the ground. Bryce wheeled around and pumped his twelve-gauge shotgun into the head of the fierce pit bull. Two other dogs pounced on Bryce, dropping his gun, and Jamie started to shoot the dog but was hit from behind by the other pit bull. She dropped her gun. Jamie quickly picked up a shovel that had fallen out of Bryce's truck, frantically swinging it back and forth, trying to keep the pit bull at bay. Bryce had grabbed one of the pit bulls by the leg and squeezed. The dog's leg broke. Then he threw the dog toward the other dog, knocking it over. The gang members had Bryce and Jamie in a circle with their guns ready to kill them. One of the gang members called the pit bulls. Bryce stood there panting and bleeding, shouting at the gangs members, "What are you waiting for, you pussies?"

Jamie was also spent, standing there, gripping the shovel and wiping the sweat out of her eyes.

One of the gang members, his name was Boxer, called out to Doberman, "We got them." Boxer put his Uzi in Bryce's back and said, "Walk now." They put a gun to the heads of both of Jamie and Bryce and told them to get up and walk. Both were bleeding from the dog bites. When they arrived at the end of the warehouse, Doberman appeared with a dog leash in his hand and a Uzi in the other. He yelled out, "Put them in the dog pen."

The dog pen was at eight-foot chain-link fence with barbed wire around the top. The pen itself was about fifty-by-one-hundred feet. There were several dog houses and individual pens. They were all about ten-by-ten1 pens. Dozens of chains hung around the pen's dog collars attached for other pit bulls were growling and barking in the pen.

Jamie whispered to Bryce, "This must be a dog fighting pen."

Doberman came up from behind Jamie and Bryce and shouted at Jamie, "Shut your mouth, bitch!" Doberman then pulled the chain that was attached to Bryce and yelled to his gang to tie Bryce's hands above his head, pointing to a pole lying on the ground. He then walked away.

As Bryce was walking, two of the pit bulls were walking right behind him, growling the whole time. The other pit bull was behind Jamie. They took them to the dog pen and put a dog collar on them that was chained to the dog pen. It was done without a struggle. Bryce quietly gripped the bar his hands were tied to. Then Doberman pulled on another chain, and Bryce's mother appeared. His blood started to boil. Bryce his rage was rising.

Doberman walked over and chained his mother to the dog pen. He walked back over to Bryce and said, "Why won't you die? But you are going to die now. But first you're going to watch your mother die first."

Doberman walked over to his mother and said, "I will make it quick for you, but your son is going to suffer a lot." He pulled out his gold plated .357 Magnum, unzipped his pants, and started peeing on Mrs. Hix.

Jamie and Bryce shouted and screamed at him to stop.

He said, "It's a shame to kill him. He has a special talent."

Amy Hix raised her head, looked into Doberman's eyes, and whispered, "He gets it from me." She reached up and grabbed him by the balls and penis and squeezed with everything she had. She too had a powerful grip like her son.

Dobermans knees buckled. He screamed with great pain, paralyzed by Amy's grip. She tried to rip Dobermans balls out of his body. He fainted and fell on Amy. Doberman was lying on top of Amy. She pulled the gun from his hand, pointed at the chain that was holding Bryce's hands above his head, missing the first shot. But Amy was dead-on on the second shot, hitting the chain and dropping Bryce to the ground. Bryce then rolled toward Jamie as Amy continued to fire randomly in the direction of the other gang members, sending them running for cover. Bryce freed Jamie. Then they both jumped behind Doberman and Amy. Bryce pushed Doberman off Amy, using his limp body as a shield. As Bryce held Doberman on his side, Jamie checked his pockets for another clip to his gun.

Bryce said sarcastically to his mother, "Took you two shots to free me, Mom. Must be slipping." He chuckled.

She answered back, "You tried shooting with a 250-pound guy lying on you?"

"Nice comeback," said Jamie.

The other gang members were reluctant to fire on Bryce and Jamie and Amy for fear of hitting their leader.

Jamie whispered, "What's the next move? Eventually, they will work their way behind us."

Bryce answered while panting, struggling to keep Doberman on his side, "I don't know what to do. You have any ideas?"

Suddenly, gunfire erupted from behind them. It was Officer Jones and Randy firing at the other dogs. The gun battle was all on again. Amy put the gun in his hand. She whispered, "Behind you."

Bryce rolled away and blew the head off the gang member. Another started to shoot Jamie when Officer Jones came running in and yelled, "Hey." The gunman turned, and Officer Jones dropped him with one shot to the head. Another gang member appeared from behind a dog box and aimed his gun toward Amy. Bryce, seeing the gunman, tried to dive across his mother, but Randy Bell fired three shots at the gunman, hitting him twice before the gang member fell. He emptied his gun toward Randy and Bryce, hitting Randy in the shoulder. Bryce covered his mother like a blanket, but he was shot while shielding his mother.

Police sirens were racing down the warehouse. The other dogs fled at the back, leaving a brutal gun battle and maybe a dying leader. As the police arrived to clean up the mess, Bryce rolled Doberman over and grabbed him around the neck, but before he could break it, Officer Jones hit him with his gun in the back of the head.

Bryce crumpled to the ground.

Jamie yelled, "What are you doing!"

Officer Jones said, "If Doberman is still alive, he is going to jail. I'm not going to let him kill him. He will pay for everything he has done. It has been a long time coming."

Two ambulances arrived. One of them took Doberman. It had three police cars following close behind. The other stayed and treated Bryce, Jamie, and his mother. Randy, who was also shot, was treated and released. It had just grazed him.

Officer Jones sat down beside Bryce and Jamie and said, "You have to go downtown after they release you. You're in my custody now."

Jamie said, "What do you mean?"

He answered, "Well, he stole his truck out of the impound yard and broke out of a hospital while in custody of the police in a small city outside of town."

While rubbing the back of his head, Bryce said, "You mean, I am arrested."

Jones answered, "Well, let's just say we have a few things to clear up, but with your testimony, we will make sure Doberman never walks the streets again, if he lives, of course. And by the way, your mother did that to him. She has quite a grip."

Bryce answered, "Where do you think I got mine from? What about my mom? She needs to get back to the cancer center."

Amy was sitting in the ambulance. Jamie walked over to the ambulance. Amy was sitting in. Jamie watched the paramedic finish, then sat down next to Amy, smiling.

Jamie said, "I have never seen anything like that." She laughed. "You almost ripped his balls right off."

Amy said, "Well, he had it coming. I guess the big dog just got neutered."

Jamie burst into laughter as the ambulance pulled away.

Officer Jones told Bryce, "You will ride with me. We will go by the hospital and have you checked out before we find a safe place to keep you."

While they were driving, Bryce just stared out the window of the police car. Bryce didn't say a word. When Officer Jones and Bryce arrived at the hospital, a male nurse with a wheelchair and two armed security officers were waiting for Bryce. The nurse helped Bryce get into the wheelchair and took him inside to see the attending physician in the emergency room. At the hospital, while Bryce and Jamie were being taken cared of, his mother was sitting in the waiting room waiting for a ride back to the cancer center.

Officer Jones brought her a cup of coffee and sat down beside her. He was staring into his cup of coffee, thinking what to say when she said, "Do you have something on your mind?"

"Yes," he said. "When your husband died some thirty years ago, his neck was broken. The investigation was unclear. Based on what I have seen today, the report I read seemed to think your son did it in a fight with him. It read that he was unconscious and didn't remember a thing. I know he was very young at the time, I just wonder."

She spoke up. "You're asking me if I killed my husband. Is this on the record or off the record."

He said, "It's off the record. The statute of limitations has run out."

"I wasn't taking any more beatings from that man, and when I woke from consciousness, my husband, Bryce's father, was choking him. At that time our hands were about the same size, they naturally thought it was him, so I let them when they told me there would be no charges because he was a minor, and under the circumstances, I let them think what they wanted. I was beaten to a pulp. Bryce was unconscious and couldn't remember what happened. He was eight years old. They weren't going to put him in jail for saving his mom's life, so they closed the case. The psychiatrist told the police he had blocked it out of his mind, and that was good enough for them. I would have came forward if anything was going to happen to him, but there was no need, so I didn't."

Officer Jones said, "Did you murder your husband?"

She replied, "Let's just say I squeezed a zit until it popped. He was a drunk, a wife beater, and when he started punching Bryce, that was the last straw for me."

He said, "There is a lot of anger in you, isn't there?"

She replied, "We have had a hard life."

Officer Jones just nodded his head and patted her on the back.

The cancer treatment research van had arrived to take her back. She asked him to tell her son she was leaving. She was very tired.

He told her he would and to get some rest.

*****

In a nearby operating room, a very skilled surgeon was trying to put Doberman back together. After a couple hours of surgery, Officer Jones was waiting for the doctor to come out, and when he did, he asked the doctor, "Will he make it?"

The doctor said, "The next couple of days will tell, but he probably will never reproduce or may never have sex. He was pretty bad. We did the best we could do. Time will tell."

Officer Jones asked, "How long of a recovery time?"

The doctor answered, "Maybe a few weeks, maybe longer. I can't tell right now. I will know more in a few days if he gets all the swelling down."

Jones turned to a uniformed officer and said, "I want a twenty-four hour guard on this room and wherever Doberman is."

Officer Jones went down the hallway, to the next floor to see Jamie. She was about to leave. She had twelve stitches in her arm and eighteen stitches in her leg from the dog bites. She was in a lot of pain. Randy and their father Rock were ready to take her home when she asked Officer Jones where Bryce is.

He answered, "We put him in a holding cell for his own protection. We have to keep him there. And his mom has two police uniformed officers outside her door. Everything is covered, so go home and get some rest."

*****

About three days later Officer Jones went to the holding cell where Bryce was. He opened the door and went inside and said, "It looks like everything has calmed down, so let's go see your mother. Jamie will meet us there."

*****

As they drove over, an old woman appeared at the hospital where Doberman was. She wanted to see him. She said she was his mother, and if the police would not let her see him, she'd come back with her lawyer. So the police officer let her see him. The police officer patted the old woman down, then escorted her inside the room. The old woman walked right up to him and held his hand very tightly and said, "I am here, baby. I am here."

Doberman's eyes opened. He tried to say something. She leaned down and listened. Only the old woman could hear what Doberman was saying.

The officer said, "Ma'am, we need to cut this short."

She said, "Okay." Then she kissed her son on the head and left the room.

The young officer then called Officer Jones and told him Doberman had a visitor and it was his mother.

Officer Jones snapped back at the young officer, "His mother is dead. Is she still there?"

"No," the young officer answered.

"Well, if she comes back, hold her and call me," Officer Jones said.

As Bryce and Officer Jones were going to the cancer center, they hardly spoke a word.

Jones said, "How are they treating you?"

"Fine," he replied as they stepped out of the elevator.

Jones then said, "Your mom is a quite interesting lady. What do you remember about your father's death?"

Bryce glared at Officer Jones for a few seconds, then blurted out, "Not much, I blacked out."

When they walked into the room, there was Jamie and her father standing around Mrs. Hix's bed, talking. Bryce walked over and gave his mother a hug and kiss. They exchanged the usual pleasantries, "How are you doing? Are the treatments working?" that sort of thing.

He got up and gave Jamie a kiss and said, "I miss you."

She replied, "The same."

After an hour or so passed, Randy showed up and came into the room and started talking with Officer Jones, so they were all there.

A few minutes later they heard a helicopter landing on the roof.

Bryce said, "I haven't heard a helicopter landing here before."

Jamie said to Bryce, "Your mom is dying for a Diet Coke."

Bryce just nodded his head and said, "I'll go down to the coffee shop and get her one."

Then everyone wanted a Coke too, so Randy offered to go along and help.

They didn't say much in the elevator ride until Randy broke the ice and said, "You know there's not much I can do about you. I don't like you, and you don't like me, but I will do my best to get along with you if you do the same." Randy extended his hand.

Bryce made a fist and said, "Give me knucks."

Their two fists collided gently. They both smiled. Then all of a sudden they could hear what sounded like gunfire. They both ran back to the elevator. They kept pushing the button, but the elevator would not respond, as if it was stuck. They took the stairs and ran twelve flights.

*****

Upstairs on the top floor the dogs had stolen a medical helicopter. They had taken Doberman and wheeled him down the hall and opened the door of Amy Hix's room. He raised up and started firing his Uzi, spraying bullets all over the room, Rock jumped onto Amy using his body as a shield. Both Jamie and Officer Jones were hit by gunfire. Nothing fatal but shot just the same. Rock took four bullets in the back. The dogs then took their leader back to the elevator they had held and went to the roof to make their escape as Bryce and Randy arrived from the stairs out of breath. They kicked open the door. They saw Officer Jones and Jamie struggling to get up and Jamie's father was lying on top of Bryce's mother. Officer Jones pointed to the roof. Bryce shouted for them to stay as he started out the door. Jamie threw him her gun. He raced up the final staircase and kicked open the door of the roof. He could see the helicopter starting to takeoff. He ran as fast as he could and leaped and grabbed the legs of the helicopter, dropping the pistol Jamie had given him. He thought, *Now what?*

As the helicopter lifted off, the door opened. Bryce could see hands waving around, so Bryce swung himself to the open door and grabbed one of the hands. It was one of the dogs but not the one he wanted, so Bryce just let him drop. Doberman looked out the open helicopter door and screamed as he watched them fall to the ground. Doberman then turned to the pilot, but Bryce had swung up again and grabbed Doberman's hand and pulled him out. Doberman had his weapon in his hand.

He shouted, "Don't you drop me. I will kill you before you do."

Bryce shouted back, "You shoot me and you're dead."

They stared at one another for a few of seconds.

Bryce then said, "Go fetch, dog," and tossed Doberman away.

Doberman opened fire on Bryce. Bryce swung back and forth, trying to avoid the gunfire as Doberman was falling. Doberman missed Bryce but hit the helicopter pilot. The helicopter was spiraling out of control toward a nearby river. All Bryce could do was hang on.

*****

Back in the hospital room doctors were tending to Jamie and Officer Jones while Randy just held his father.

His father said to him, "I don't think I am going to make it, so there are a few things that need to be said."

A doctor was trying to stop the bleeding.

He grabbed Randy by the shirt and pulled him close. "I cheated you and Bryce. I spiked his drink to get him disqualified. I did it for you at the time." He then coughed a couple times. "I did not think of what it would do to him. I panicked. Can you forgive me?"

Randy did not know what to say he just rubbed the side of his face. "Why? Why?" was all he could say.

His father took one last breath and said, "Because I love you, son. I was wrong. You have to make it right. You make it right!" His eyes rolled back into his head, and he died.

The doctors tried CPR, but it did no good. He was gone.

Jamie just sat on the floor, crying, and Randy just stared at the ceiling. Jamie was taken away. She had a bullet in her shoulder, and Officer Jones had a bullet in his leg and his side. Remarkably, Amy had not been hit. Rock's body had saved her. She kept asking, "Where is Bryce?" over and over again. So Randy went to the roof, but nothing was there. A few drops of blood was all he could find.

*****

The helicopter had crashed into the channel. No one had even seen it hit the water. Bryce was treading water. He could feel a burning in his side. He grabbed hold of a nearby garbage barge, pulled himself up onto the barge and just lay there. He said a little prayer to God.

He said, "God, please don't take me now. Please give me a chance for true happiness. Someone loves me, and I can love her. I'm just asking for a chance." He then passed out.

A few hours later the sun came up. A barge worker poked at Bryce to see if he would move. Bryce opened his eyes.

"Hey, he is alive." The worker called out to his boss with the radio and said that they have a man who appears to be shot on the barge. "Would you send the Coast Guard to pick him up?"

The Coast Guard arrived. The medic on board took care of Bryce and told him he would be fine. They asked him what it happened, and Bryce told them. A few phone calls were made. One finally made it to Jamie, telling her he was fine.

Bryce was taken in an ambulance. The EMT checked Bryce over, cleaned his cut on his side, and bandaged it. Bryce told the EMT to take him to the cancer research center. The EMT shook his head and said we have to go to our hospital. Bryce grabbed him around the hand and squeezed and said, "Please."

The EMT shouted to the driver, "Take us to the cancer research center now."

The driver shouted back, "Okay, you're the boss," as they sped away.

The ambulance arrived at the hospital, Jamie and Officer Jones were downstairs, about to be transported to the hospital for observation. Bryce had jumped out of the ambulance and went inside. Jamie was sitting in a wheelchair. Bryce ran to her side, dropping to his knees. Emotionally, he said, "Are you okay?"

Jamie rubbed the back of Bryce's head and said, "I'll be fine." But with quivering lips, Jamie told Bryce what happened and that her father had died and how he had saved his mother's life and that they had found Doberman's body. He was dead from a fall.

Bryce told her how Doberman died. He then said, "Your father saved my mother. I wish I could have thanked him." Bryce road in the ambulance with Jamie to the hospital.

When they arrived at the hospital, Bryce asked Jamie if it would be okay if he borrowed her cell phone. He wanted to call his mom while the doctor was examining her. Bryce called his mom.

She answered, "Hello."

Bryce said, "It's me."

A sigh of relief came over Amy Hicks.

"I'm sorry, Mom, I rode with Jamie to the hospital. She told me what happened, and that you were fine." He then sighed and said, "So her dad saved your life. I never saw that coming."

Amy replied, "Rock was a good man that made a mistake a long time ago. I hope you can forgive him and put these bitter feelings to rest and move on with your life."

Bryce answered, "Mom, he saved your life. How could I not forgive him?"

Amy then said, "Come see me later. Make sure Jamie is fine. Be supportive. After all, she just lost her father."

Bryce agreed, told his mom that he loved her, and hung up the phone.

About an hour later, Jamie was released from the hospital. The doctor told her to go home and rest and call if she had any problems. Bryce then called a cab to take them to Jamie's place.

As they arrived at Jamie's, they helped each other into the house and sat on the couch. She said that her father's funeral will be in a few days and that almost all the dogs have been rounded up. "The word on the street is you're safe now, so what are you going to do?"

Bryce looked at Jaime and said, "What do you mean?"

She said, "Are you going to stay when your mother's treatment is over, or are you going home?"

Bryce paused and said, "I never even thought about that. I guess some discussion between you and me about the future has to happen."

Jaime nodded her head. Her lips quivered. "Would you stay here with me?"

Bryce asked Jaime, "Would you consider going home with me?"

Neither got the answer they wanted.

Jaime said, "Let's just put this on the back burner till your mother is well."

Bryce nodded and said, "Okay."

Bryce and Jamie sat on the couch and just held each other. Jamie stared at the ground as Bryce stared at the ceiling. The embrace was long and silent for Bryce. It felt like it was their last embrace. Bryce was always the pessimist. To Jamie it felt like good-bye, but the optimist in Jamie believed there was still hope. She refused her negative feelings, thinking, *Bryce loves me. He won't let me go.*

*****

Back at the gym Randy was sitting in his office staring at the two gold medals in a glass case on his wall, knowing in his heart what he must do. It would be the right thing because what his father said,

"Make it right," kept going over and over at the back of his mind. He tapped his head on the back of his chair, just staring.

"My sister loves Bryce, and I hate him. My father is gone, and I'm here trying to make sense of his words, 'Make it right. Make it right.' Thanks, Dad."

Randy was sitting in his chair. He pushed himself over to his dad's desk. There on the desk was a rock, a gift from Jamie when she was eight years old. Painted on the rock, it said, "I love you, Dad, from Jamie." Randy remembered going down to the beach with Jamie to help her find the perfect rock. It took her hours to till Jamie settled on this one. As Jamie carefully painted the rock, he remembered telling Jamie, "This is a stupid gift." But how proud his dad was of that rock. He kept it on his desk all these years. Randy picked the rock up and tossed up the air a few times. He then threw the rock at the glass case displaying his gold medals, shattering the case as the medals fell to the ground.

*****

Two days later, on a cloudy and rainy day, at the funeral of his father, Randy was going to make it right. After the service Randy reached out to hug his sister. He then looked at Bryce and extended his fist. They fist bumped.

Randy glared at Bryce, then spoke. "I respect you as an opponent. You're the only man who ever beat me in anything. My father made a great mistake a long time ago. I know this won't ease all the pain and suffering that my father caused you and your bitterness about this great country of ours." Randy handed him his first gold medal.

Bryce's eyes opened wide, staring at Randy.

Randy said, "You earned this, not only by defeating me but saving my sister several times. Take this medal. You earned this long time ago."

Before Bryce could speak, two men walked up. One of them said, "Pardon me for this intrusion on this sad day, but I would like to talk with all three of you." He then showed his badge and introduced himself. "I am special agent Birch, and this is special agent Hale. I know this is not a good time, but time is slipping away, and the sooner we get started, the better it will be."

As Officer Jones walked up, he said, "Let's talk over here."

Bryce and Jamie were puzzled about what was going on, but they walked over to a big oak tree.

The agent started speaking and told them how all they have tracked a terrorist and drug ring to the gang of the dogs. "They were involved in several plots and cover-ups for drugs and terrorist activities. Although Doberman is dead, he was just one of many links to a bigger organization. We would like you to join our team to help rid this country of this scum. I have already talked to your captain, and he is willing to give you a two-year leave of absence. You will receive special training, and you will be doing your country a great favor. So think it over. I will call you in forty-eight hours."

Both agents shook the hands of all of them and left the cemetery in a big black car.

Officer Jones said, "That invitation was to all of us, or even just one or two of us it's not an all-or-nothing deal. It's a great chance to really make a difference."

Bryce said, "I am a brick mason, not a police officer. I've had no training for this."

Randy said, "What the hell would they want with me or him?" He pointed at Bryce.

Officer Jones said, "They have been watching us and the work that we've done on this case and with the contacts we have here. They think we can get all of the gang members and the ones that are tied to terrorist organizations. It's a great opportunity for all of us or some of us." He was looking right at Bryce when he said that.

Bryce could tell he was talking about Jamie and himself.

Bryce stood up and said, "Well, I have to go to the research hospital. I have a meeting with my mother's doctor. He has the results from her tests."

Jamie said, "I will go with you."

As they rode in Bryce's truck, Jamie went on and on about the tremendous opportunity this was, that this was something she had always dreamed of.

Bryce kept listening to her. He could tell this was something she wanted to do. Jaime had hardly even mentioned the gold medal her brother gave him. Bryce was feeling distant for the first time.

As they arrived at the center, Jamie realized she had dominated the conversation the whole ride from the cemetery. She sighed and reached for Bryce's hand and asked him if anything was wrong.

Bryce shrugged his shoulders and said, "I guess I am just a little worried about the meeting with the doctor."

As they walked to his office, Bryce was very nervous. He was glad Jamie was with him. The receptionists asked for their names. They told them to wait in the waiting room. After about five minutes, they called for Bryce to enter the office. He went in. The doctor shook his hand and told him to sit down. He did.

The doctor said, "This is never easy, but I'll give it to you straight. We did all we could. We just couldn't get it all."

He asked, "What does that mean?"

The doctor answered, "Your mother has little time left."

"How much time?" Bryce asked.

"A year or maybe two. It's hard to say. The treatment just didn't work. She is very weak right now, but she will get stronger, and then her condition will weaken her again. My suggestion is to take her home. Let her do anything she wants. To go to Paris or Vegas. Go see places while she still has the strength. I'm sorry, Mr. Hix." The doctor placed his hand on Bryce's shoulder. "You can take a few minutes in here if you need to. I have other patients to see." He paused, then left his office.

A single tear rolled down Bryce's face. He then got up from the chair and walked into the waiting room. Jamie stood up, and she could see in his face that the news was bad. She ran over to him and hugged him. Without saying a word, she just held him.

Bryce finally spoke. "I need to see my mom, probably alone."

"Okay," she said. She pulled back and nodded. "I'll be at home.

Call me, I'll come over and we will sit with your mother. If you want this, let me know, okay?"

He pulled away and took to the stairs to his mom, for he did not know what to say. He stood in front of her door for a minute, trying to get himself together. He opened the door. His mother was sitting on the bed fully dressed, and her suitcase was packed. His eyes were red and watery. He had a puzzled look on his face.

She spoke before he could say anything. "I want to go home as soon as possible. Can we start tonight?"

He nodded his head and said, "Okay, Mom, we will leave tonight. Do you care if I see Jamie on the way out?"

She replied, "Is she not coming with us, I thought..."

Bryce just shook his head no.

They loaded up Bryce's truck and drove to Jamie's house. He told his mother about the great opportunity for her and how he could not ask her to give up a dream job for him.

They drove to her house. Jamie came running out and opened the door for his mother and hugged her and said, "Come in that may fix you something."

Amy said, "No, thanks, I'm a little tired. I'll just sit here a while."

A surprised look came over Jamie's face.

Bryce stepped out and said, "Let's talk a minute inside, okay?"

A worried look came over her face as he walked into the house. He took a deep breath and said, "Jamie, my mom wants to go home now. I know this isn't how I want to talk to you, but she has little time left."

Jaime just stood there with tears running down her face. She said, "What about us?"

Bryce answered, "I have waited so long to be happy. I can wait a little longer. You have a new job that you want to do. It is a dream of yours. You got to do it, or you will regret it for the rest of your life."

She reached out and hugged him, saying, "No, no, I need you. I love you!"

Bryce smiled and said, "You don't know how long I have waited for someone to say that to me. But listen, you go do your job, and I will wait for you. I have been waiting all my life for you, another year or two won't matter. But if for some reason in the next year or two, you change your mind about me, don't call me or write me a dear John letter, just let me believe that someday you will come back to me. I would rather live the rest of my life hoping for happiness than wait a few years with none."

Jaime just squeezed him harder and harder. She pulled back. They stared into each other's eyes and at the same time said, "I love you."

He said, "I have to go. Call me or write me, but please don't forget me!"

As Bryce left the house and got into his wrecked and bullet-hole-ridden truck, all Jaime could do was wave. As he drove away, she suddenly had an irresistible feeling. Jaime needed to say something. She rushed to her car, but Jaime had locked her keys inside.

*****

Bryce was driving now on the interstate, heading out of town. He heard a siren behind him. He thought, *What now?* He pulled over. A highway patrolman got out of his car and walked up to the truck. The patrolman looked at the truck over, putting his finger in a few of the bullet holes.

The patrolman said to Bryce, "This truck has been shot to hell, and it looks like it's been rolled."

Bryce answered, saying sarcastically, "I had a bad week."

The patrolman chuckled and said, "License and insurance, please."

Bryce said, "I wasn't speeding."

His mother said, "What did we do?"

The patrolman just repeated the question.

Bryce now was steaming with anger and muttering to himself, "I can't wait to get out of this town."

Then another police car showed up. It was Officer Jones. He stepped out and walked up to his truck and said, "In trouble again, Bryce?"

Bryce just raised his head and said, "Can you get me out of this? We really want to go home."

"No, I can't do that. I believe you're going to have to answer a few questions before you leave, so step out of the car and come back to mine."

Bryce got out of his truck, bitching and griping all the way to the car.

Officer Jones told Bryce, "We have a complaint against you. The victim is sitting in the back seat of my car."

Then the door opened, and Jamie stepped out. She said, "This man is a thief," in a soft voice. He stole my heart." She hugged him. She whispered in Bryce's ear, "They gave me two weeks off. I'd love to see where you live." Jamie kissed Bryce, then said, "Grab my bag out of the car."

Bryce did.

Jamie then said, "Don't forget these." She tossed him her handcuffs!

His mother said, "What are those for, Bryce?"

He just smiled.

*****

Meanwhile, back in the city, a secret meeting was being held. The new leader of the dogs had every member left there. He talked about the future and how the dogs would be stronger than ever. They have expanded not only in the US but other countries as well, and the first order of business was to settle all old debts. "Bryce Hix must die. Police officers Jones and Bell must die. Our new partners will pay well for information and violent acts against the police and federal agencies like the FBI and the CIA. Welcome to the new dogs. I am your new leader. Older brother of Doberman. My dog name is the Great Dane."

The End
Or is it?

Milton Keynes UK
Ingram Content Group UK Ltd.
UKHW050826250324
439991UK00001B/236